T0145670

The Devil's Paw

The Devil's Paw

E. Phillips Oppenheim

MINT EDITIONS

The Devil's Paw was first published in 1920.

This edition published by Mint Editions 2021.

ISBN 9781513281247 | E-ISBN 9781513286266

Published by Mint Editions®

MINT
EDITIONS

minteditionbooks.com

Publishing Director: Jennifer Newens
Design & Production: Rachel Lopez Metzger
Project Manager: Micaela Clark
Typesetting: Westchester Publishing Services

Contents

I

The two men, sole occupants of the somewhat shabby cottage parlour, lingered over their port, not so much with the air of wine lovers, but rather as human beings and intimates, perfectly content with their surroundings and company. Outside, the wind was howling over the marshes, and occasional bursts of rain came streaming against the window panes. Inside at any rate was comfort, triumphing over varying conditions. The cloth upon the plain deal table was of fine linen, the decanter and glasses were beautifully cut; there were walnuts and, in a far corner, cigars of a well-known brand and cigarettes from a famous tobacconist. Beyond that little oasis, however, were all the evidences of a hired abode. A hole in the closely drawn curtains was fastened together by a safety pin. The horsehair easy-chairs bore disfiguring antimacassars, the photographs which adorned the walls were grotesque but typical of village ideals, the carpet was threadbare, the closed door secured by a latch instead of the usual knob. One side of the room was littered with golf clubs, a huge game bag and several boxes of cartridges. Two shotguns lay upon the remains of a sofa. It scarcely needed the costume of Miles Furley, the host, to demonstrate the fact that this was the temporary abode of a visitor to the Blakeney marshes in search of sport.

Furley, broad-shouldered, florid, with tanned skin and grizzled hair, was still wearing the high sea boots and jersey of the duck shooter. His companion, on the other hand, a tall, slim man, with high forehead, clear eyes, stubborn jaw, and straight yet sensitive mouth, wore the ordinary dinner clothes of civilisation. The contrast between the two men might indeed have afforded some ground for speculation as to the nature of their intimacy. Furley, a son of the people, had the air of cultivating, even clinging to a certain plebeian strain, never so apparent as when he spoke, or in his gestures. He was a Member of Parliament for a Labour constituency, a shrewd and valuable exponent of the gospel of the working man. What he lacked in the higher qualities of oratory he made up in sturdy common sense. The will-o'-the-wisp Socialism of the moment, with its many attendant "isms" and theories, received scant favour at his hands. He represented the solid element in British Labour politics, and it was well known that he had refused a seat in the Cabinet in order to preserve an absolute independence. He had a remarkable gift of taciturnity, which in a man of his class made for strength, and it was concerning him that the Prime Minister had made his famous epigram, that Furley was the Labour man whom he feared the most and dreaded the least.

Julian Orden, with an exterior more promising in many respects than that of his friend, could boast of no similar distinctions. He was the youngest son of a particularly fatuous peer resident in the neighbourhood, had started life as a barrister, in which profession he had attained a moderate success, had enjoyed a brief but not inglorious spell of soldiering, from which he had retired slightly lamed for life, and had filled up the intervening period in the harmless occupation of censoring. His friendship with Furley appeared on the surface too singular to be anything else but accidental. Probably no one save the two men themselves understood it, and they both possessed the gift of silence.

"What's all this peace talk mean?" Julian Orden asked, fingering the stem of his wineglass.

"Who knows?" Furley grunted. "The newspapers must have their daily sensation."

"I have a theory that it is being engineered."

"Bolo business, eh?"

Julian Orden moved in his place a little uneasily. His long, nervous fingers played with the stick which stood always by the side of his chair.

"You don't believe in it, do you?" he asked quietly.

Furley looked straight ahead of him. His eyes seemed caught by the glitter of the lamplight upon the cut-glass decanter.

"You know my opinion of war, Julian," he said. "It's a filthy, intolerable heritage from generations of autocratic government. No democracy ever wanted war. Every democracy needs and desires peace."

"One moment," Julian interrupted. "You must remember that a democracy seldom possesses the imperialistic spirit, and a great empire can scarcely survive without it."

"Arrant nonsense!" was the vigorous reply. "A great empire, from hemisphere to hemisphere, can be kept together a good deal better by democratic control. Force is always the arriere pensee of the individual and the autocrat."

"These are generalities," Julian declared. "I want to know your opinion about a peace at the present moment."

"Not having any, thanks. You're a dilettante journalist by your own confession, Julian, and I am not going to be drawn."

"There is something in it, then?"

"Maybe," was the careless admission. "You're a visitor worth having, Julian. '70 port and homegrown walnuts! A nice little addition to my simple fare! Must you go back to-morrow?"

Julian nodded.

"We've another batch of visitors coming,—Stenson amongst them, by the bye."

Furley nodded. His eyes narrowed, and little lines appeared at their corners.

"I can't imagine," he confessed. "What brings Stenson down to Maltenby. I should have thought that your governor and he could scarcely spend ten minutes together without quarrelling!"

"They never do spend ten minutes together alone," Julian replied drily. "I see to that. Then my mother, you know, has the knack of getting interesting people together. The Bishop is coming, amongst others. And, Furley, I wanted to ask you—do you know anything of a young woman—she is half Russian, I believe—who calls herself Miss Catherine Abbeway?"

"Yes, I know her," was the brief rejoinder.

"She lived in Russia for some years, it seems," Julian continued. "Her mother was Russian—a great writer on social subjects."

Furley nodded.

"Miss Abbeway is rather that way herself," he remarked. "I've heard her lecture in the East End. She has got hold of the woman's side of the Labour question as well as any one I ever came across."

"She is a most remarkably attractive young person," Julian declared pensively.

"Yes, she's good-looking. A countess in her own right, they tell me, but she keeps her title secret for fear of losing influence with the working classes. She did a lot of good down Poplar way. Shouldn't have thought she'd have been your sort, Julian."

"Why?"

"Too serious."

Julian smiled—rather a peculiar, introspective smile.

"I, too, can, be serious sometimes," he said.

His friend thrust his hands into his trousers pocket and, leaning back in his chair, looked steadfastly at his guest.

"I believe you can, Julian," he admitted. "Sometimes I am not quite sure that I understand you. That's the worst of a man with the gift for silence."

"You're not a great talker yourself," the younger man reminded his host.

"When you get me going on my own subject," Furley remarked, "I find it hard to stop, and you are a wonderful listener. Have you got any views of your own? I never hear them."

Julian drew the box of cigarettes towards him.

"Oh, yes, I've views of my own," he confessed. "Some day, perhaps, you shall know what they are."

"A man of mystery!" his friend jeered good-naturedly.

Julian lit his cigarette and watched the smoke curl upward.

"Let's talk about the duck," he suggested.

The two men sat in silence for some minutes. Outside, the storm seemed to have increased in violence. Furley rose, threw a log on to the fire and resumed his place.

"Geese flew high," he remarked.

"Too high for me," Julian confessed.

"You got one more than I did."

"Sheer luck. The outside bird dipped down to me."

Furley filled his guest's glass and then his own.

"What on earth have you kept your shooting kit on for?" the latter asked, with lazy curiosity.

Furley glanced down at his incongruous attire and seemed for a moment ill at ease.

"I've got to go out presently," he announced.

Julian raised his eyebrows.

"Got to go out?" he repeated. "On a night like this? Why, my dear fellow—"

He paused abruptly. He was a man of quick perceptions, and he realised his host's embarrassment. Nevertheless, there was an awkward pause in the conversation. Furley rose to his feet and frowned. He fetched a jar of tobacco from a shelf and filled his pouch deliberately:

"Sorry to seem mysterious, old chap," he said. "I've just a bit of a job to do. It doesn't amount to anything, but—well, it's the sort of affair we don't talk about much."

"Well, you're welcome to all the amusement you'll get out of it, a night like this."

Furley laid down his pipe, ready-filled, and drank off his port.

"There isn't much amusement left in the world, is there, just now?" he remarked gravely.

"Very little indeed. It's three years since I handled a shotgun before to-night."

"You've really chucked the censoring?"

"Last week. I've had a solid year at it."

"Fed up?"

"Not exactly that. My own work accumulated so."

"Briefs coming along, eh?"

"I'm a sort of hack journalist as well, as you reminded me just now," Julian explained a little evasively.

"I wonder you stuck at the censoring so long. Isn't it terribly tedious?"

"Sometimes. Now and then we come across interesting things, though. For instance, I discovered a most original cipher the other day."

"Did it lead to anything?" Furley asked curiously.

"Not at present. I discovered it, studying a telegram from Norway. It was addressed to a perfectly respectable firm of English timber merchants who have an office in the city. This was the original: 'Fir planks too narrow by half.' Sounds harmless enough, doesn't it?"

"Absolutely. What's the hidden meaning?"

"There I am still at a loss," Julian confessed, "but treated with the cipher it comes out as 'Thirty-eight steeple on barn.'"

Furley stared for a moment, then he lit his pipe.

"Well, of the two," he declared, "I should prefer the first rendering for intelligibility."

"So would most people," Julian assented, smiling, "yet I am sure there is something in it—some meaning, of course, that needs a context to grasp it."

"Have you interviewed the firm of timber merchants?"

"Not personally. That doesn't come into my department. The name of the man who manages the London office, though, is Fenn—Nicholas Fenn."

Furley withdrew the pipe from his mouth. His eyebrows had come together in a slight frown.

"Nicholas Fenn, the Labour M.P.?"

"That's the fellow. You know him, of course?"

"Yes, I know him," Furley replied thoughtfully. "He is secretary of the Timber Trades Union and got in for one of the divisions of Hull last year."

"I understand that there is nothing whatever against him personally," Julian continued, "although as a politician he is of course beneath contempt. He started life as a village schoolmaster and has worked his way up most creditably. He professed to understand the cable as it appeared in its original form. All the same, it's very odd that, treated by a cipher which I got on the track of a few days previously, this same message should work out as I told you."

"Of course," Furley observed, "ciphers can lead you—"

He stopped short. Julian, who had been leaning over towards the cigarette bog, glanced around at his friend. There was a frown on Furley's forehead. He withdrew his pipe from between his teeth.

"What did you say you made of it?" he demanded.

"'Thirty-eight steeple on barn.'"

"Thirty-eight! That's queer!"

"Why is it queer?"

There was a moment's silence. Furley glanced at the little clock upon the mantelpiece. It was five and twenty minutes past nine.

"I don't know whether you have ever heard, Julian," he said, "that our enemies on the other side of the North Sea are supposed to have divided the whole of the eastern coast of Great Britain into small, rectangular districts, each about a couple of miles square. One of our secret service chaps got hold of a map some time ago."

"No, I never heard this," Julian acknowledged. "Well?"

"It's only a coincidence, of course," Furley went on, "but number thirty-eight happens to be the two-mile block of seacoast of which this cottage is just about the centre. It stretches to Cley on one side and Salthouse on the other, and inland as far as Dutchman's Common. I am not suggesting that there is any real connection between your cable and this fact, but that you should mention it at this particular moment—well, as I said, it's a coincidence."

"Why?"

Furley had risen to his feet. He threw open the door and listened for a moment in the passage. When he came back he was carrying some oilskins.

"Julian," he said, "I know you are a bit of a cynic about espionage and that sort of thing. Of course, there has been a terrible lot of exaggeration, and heaps of fellows go gassing about secret service jobs, all the way up the coast from here to Scotland, who haven't the least idea what the thing means. But there is a little bit of it done, and in my humble way they find me an occasional job or two down here. I won't say that anything ever comes of our efforts—we're rather like the special constables of the secret service—but just occasionally we come across something suspicious."

"So that's why you're going out again to-night, is it?"

Furley nodded.

"This is my last night. I am off up to town on Monday and sha'n't be able to get down again this season."

"Had any adventures?"

"Not the ghost of one. I don't mind admitting that I've had a good many wettings and a few scares on that stretch of marshland, but I've never seen or heard anything yet to send in a report about. It just happens, though, that to-night there's a special vigilance whip out."

"What does that mean?" Julian enquired curiously.

"Something supposed to be up," was the dubious reply. "We've a very imaginative chief, I might tell you."

"But what sort of thing could happen?" Julian persisted. "What are you out to prevent, anyway?"

Furley relit his pipe, thrust a flask into his pocket, and picked up a thick stick from a corner of the room.

"Can't tell," he replied laconically. "There's an idea, of course, that communications are carried on with the enemy from somewhere down this coast. Sorry to leave you, old fellow," he added. "Don't sit up. I never fasten the door here. Remember to look after your fire upstairs, and the whisky is on the sideboard here."

"I shall be all right, thanks," Julian assured his host. "No use my offering to come with you, I suppose?"

"Not allowed," was the brief response.

"Thank heavens!" Julian exclaimed piously, as a storm of rain blew in through the half-open door. "Good night and good luck, old chap!"

Furley's reply was drowned in the roar of wind. Julian secured the door, underneath which a little stream of rain was creeping in. Then he returned to the sitting room, threw a log upon the fire, and drew one of the ancient easy-chairs close up to the blaze.

II

Julian, notwithstanding his deliberate intention of abandoning himself to an hour's complete repose, became, after the first few minutes of solitude, conscious of a peculiar and increasing sense of restlessness. With the help of a rubber-shod stick which leaned against his chair, he rose presently to his feet and moved about the room, revealing a lameness which had the appearance of permanency. In the small, white-ceilinged apartment his height became more than ever noticeable, also the squareness of his shoulders and the lean vigour of his frame. He handled his gun for a moment and laid it down; glanced at the card stuck in the cheap looking glass, which announced that David Grice let lodgings and conducted shooting parties; turned with a shiver from the contemplation of two atrocious oleographs, a church calendar pinned upon the wall, and a battered map of the neighbourhood, back to the table at which he had been seated. He selected a cigarette and lit it. Presently he began to talk to himself, a habit which had grown upon him during the latter years of a life whose secret had entailed a certain amount of solitude.

"Perhaps," he murmured, "I am psychic. Nevertheless, I am convinced that something is happening, something not far away."

He stood for a while, listening intently, the cigarette burning away between his fingers. Then, stooping a little, he passed out into the narrow passage and opened the door into the kitchen behind, from which the woman who came to minister to their wants had some time ago departed. Everything was in order here and spotlessly neat. He climbed the narrow staircase, looked in at Furley's room and his own, and at the third apartment, in which had been rigged up a temporary bath. The result was unilluminating. He turned and descended the stairs.

"Either," he went on, with a very slight frown, "I am not psychic, or whatever may be happening is happening out of doors."

He raised the latch of the door, under which a little pool of water was now standing, and leaned out. There seemed to be a curious cessation of immediate sounds. From somewhere straight ahead of him, on the other side of that black velvet curtain of darkness, came the dull booming of the wind, tearing across the face of the marshes; and beyond it, beating time in a rhythmical sullen roar, the rise and fall of the sea upon the shingle. But near at hand, for some reason, there was almost silence.

The rain had ceased, the gale for a moment had spent itself. The strong, salty moisture was doubly refreshing after the closeness of the small, lamplit room. Julian lingered there for several moments.

"Nothing like fresh air," he muttered, "for driving away fancies."

Then he suddenly stiffened. He leaned forward into the dark, listening. This time there was no mistake. A cry, faint and pitiful though it was, reached his ears distinctly.

"Julian! Julian!"

"Coming, old chap," he shouted. "Wait until I get a torch."

He stepped quickly back into the sitting room, drew an electric torch from the drawer of the homely little chiffonier and, regardless of regulations, stepped once more out into the darkness, now pierced for him by that single brilliant ray. The door opened on to a country road filled with gleaming puddles. On the other side of the way was a strip of grass, sloping downwards; then a broad dyke, across which hung the remains of a footbridge. The voice came from the water, fainter now but still eager. Julian hurried forward, fell on his knees by the side of the dyke and, passing his hands under his friend's shoulders, dragged him out of the black, sluggish water.

"My God!" he exclaimed. "What happened, Miles? Did you slip?"

"The bridge gave way when I was half across," was the muttered response. "I think my leg's broken. I fell in and couldn't get clear—just managed to raise my head out of the water and cling to the rail."

"Hold tight," Julian enjoined. "I'm going to drag you across the road. It's the best I can do."

They reached the threshold of the sitting room.

"Sorry, old chap," faltered Furley—and fainted.

He came to himself in front of the sitting-room fire, to find his lips wet with brandy and his rescuer leaning over him. His first action was to feel his leg.

"That's all right," Julian assured him. "It isn't broken. I've been over it carefully. If you're quite comfortable, I'll step down to the village and fetch the medico. It isn't a mile away."

"Don't bother about the doctor for a moment," Furley begged. "Listen to me. Take your torch—go out and examine that bridge. Come back and tell me what's wrong with it."

"What the dickens does that matter?" Julian objected. "It's the doctor we want. The dyke's flooded, and I expect the supports gave way."

"Do as I ask," Furley insisted. "I have a reason."

Julian rose to his feet, walked cautiously to the edge of the dyke, turned on his light, and looked downwards. One part of the bridge remained; the other was caught in the weeds, a few yards down, and the single plank which formed its foundation was sawn through, clean and straight. He gazed at it for a moment in astonishment. Then he turned back towards the cottage, to receive another shock. About forty yards up the lane, drawn in close to a straggling hedge, was a small motor-car, revealed to him by a careless swing of his torch. He turned sharply towards it, keeping his torch as much concealed as possible. It was empty—a small coupe of pearl-grey—a powerful two-seater, with deep, cushioned seats and luxuriously fitted body. He flashed his torch on to the maker's name and returned thoughtfully to his friend.

"Miles," he confessed, as he entered the sitting room, "there are some things I will never make fun of again. Have you a personal enemy here?"

"Not one," replied Furley. "The soldiers, who are all decent fellows, the old farmer at the back, and your father and mother are the only people with whom I have the slightest acquaintance in these parts."

"The bridge has been deliberately sawn through," Julian announced gravely.

Furley nodded. He seemed prepared for the news.

"There is something doing in this section, then," he muttered. "Julian, will you take my job on?"

"Like a bird," was the prompt response. "Tell me exactly what to do?"

Furley sat up, still nursing his leg.

"Put on your sea boots, and your oilskins over your clothes," he directed. "You will want your own stick, so take that revolver and an electric torch. You can't get across the remains of the bridge, but about fifty yards down to the left, as you leave the door, the water's only about a foot deep. Walk through it, scramble up the other side, and come back again along the edge of the dyke until you come to the place where one lands from the broken bridge. Is that clear?"

"Entirely."

"After that, you go perfectly straight along a sort of cart track until you come to a gate. When you have passed through it, you must climb a bank on your lefthand side and walk along the top. It's a beastly path, and there are dykes on either side of you."

"Pooh!" Julian exclaimed. "You forget that I am a native of this part of the world."

"You come to a sort of stile at the end of about three hundred yards," Furley continued. "You get over that, and the bank breaks up into two. You keep to the left, and it leads you right down into the marsh. Turn seaward. It will be a nasty scramble, but there will only be about fifty yards of it. Then you get to a bit of rough ground—a bank of grass-grown sand. Below that there is the shingle and the sea. That is where you take up your post."

"Can I use my torch," Julian enquired, "and what am I to look out for?"

"Heaven knows," replied Furley, "except that there's a general suggestion of communications between some person on land and some person approaching from the sea. I don't mind confessing that I've done this job, on and off, whenever I've been down here, for a couple of years, and I've never seen or heard a suspicious thing yet. We are never told a word in our instructions, either, or given any advice. However, what I should do would be to lie flat down on the top of that bank and listen. If you hear anything peculiar, then you must use your discretion about the torch. It's a nasty job to make over to a pal, Julian, but I know you're keen on anything that looks like an adventure."

"All over it," was the ready reply. "What about leaving you alone, though, Miles?"

"You put the whisky and soda where I can get at it," Furley directed, "and I shall be all right. I'm feeling stronger every moment. I expect your sea boots are in the scullery. And hurry up, there's a good fellow. We're twenty minutes behind time, as it is."

Julian started on his adventure without any particular enthusiasm. He found the crossing, returned along the side of the bank, trudged along the cart track until he arrived at the gate, and climbed up on the dyke without misadventure. From here he made his way more cautiously, using his stick with his right hand, his torch, with his thumb upon the knob, in his left. The lull in the storm seemed to be at an end. Black, low-hanging clouds were closing in upon him. Away to the right, where the line of marshes was unbroken, the boom of the wind grew louder. A gust very nearly blew him down the bank. He was compelled to shelter for a moment on its lee side, whilst a scud of snow and sleet passed like an icy whirlwind. The roar of the sea was full in his ears now, and though he must still have been fully two hundred yards away from it, little ghostly specks of white spray were dashed, every now and then, into his face. From here he made his way with great care, almost crawling, until he came to the stile. In the marshes he was twice in salt water over his knees, but he scrambled out until he reached the grass-grown sand bank which Furley had indicated. Obeying orders, he lay down and listened intently for any fainter sounds mingled with the tumult of nature. After a few minutes, it was astonishing how his eyes found themselves able to penetrate the darkness which at first had seemed like a black wall. Some distance to the right he could make out the outline of a deserted barn, once used as a coast-guard station and now only a depository for the storing of life belts. In front of him he could trace the bank of shingle and the line of the sea, and presently the outline of some dark object, lying just out of reach of the breaking waves, attracted his attention. He watched it steadily. For some time it was as motionless as the log he presumed it to be. Then, without any warning, it hunched itself up and drew a little farther back. There was no longer any doubt. It was a human being, lying on its stomach with its head turned to the sea.

Julian, who had entered upon his adventure with the supercilious incredulity of a staunch unbeliever invited to a spiritualist's seance, was conscious for a moment of an absolutely new sensation. A person of acute psychological instincts, he found himself analysing that sensation almost as soon as it was conceived.

"There is no doubt," he confessed under his breath, "that I am afraid!"

His heart was beating with unaccustomed vigour; he was conscious of an acute tingling in all his senses. Then, still lying on his stomach, almost holding his breath, he saw the thin line of light from an electric torch steal out along the surface of the sea, obviously from the hand of his fellow watcher. Almost at that same moment the undefined agitation which had assailed him passed. He set his teeth and watched that line of light. It moved slowly sideways along the surface of the sea, as though searching for something. Julian drew himself cautiously, inch by inch, to the extremity of the sand hummock. His brain was working with a new clearness. An inspiration flashed in upon him during those few seconds. He knew the geography of the place well,—the corner of the barn, the steeple beyond, and the watcher lying in a direct line. His cipher was explained!

Perfectly cool now, Julian thought with some regret of the revolver which he had scorned to bring. He occupied himself, during these seconds of watching, by considering with care what his next action was to be. If he even set his foot upon the shingle, the watcher below would take alarm, and if he once ran away, pursuit was hopeless. The figure, so far as he could distinguish it, was more like that of a boy than a man. Julian began to calculate coolly the chances of an immediate intervention. Then things happened, and for a moment he held his breath.

The line of light had shot out once more, and this time it seemed to reveal something, something which rose out of the water and which looked like nothing so much as a long strip of zinc piping. The watcher at the edge of the sea threw down his torch and gripped the end of it, and Julian, carried away with excitement, yielded to an instant and overpowering temptation. He flashed on his own torch and watched while the eager figure seemed by some means to unscrew the top of the coil and drew from it a dark, rolled-up packet. Even at that supreme moment, the slim figure upon the beach seemed to become conscious of the illumination of which he was the centre. He swung round,—and that was just as far as Julian Orden got in his adventure. After a lapse of time, during which he seemed to live in a whirl of blackness, where a thousand men were beating at a thousand anvils, filling the world with sparks, with the sound of every one of their blows reverberating in his ears, he opened his eyes to find himself lying on his back, with one leg in a pool of salt water, which was being dashed industriously into his face by an unseen hand. By his side he was conscious of the presence of a thick-set man in a fisherman's costume of brown oilskins and a southwester pulled down as though to hide his features, obviously the man who had dealt him the blow. Then he heard a very soft, quiet voice behind him.

"He will do now. Come."

The man by his side grunted.

"I am going to make sure of him," he said thickly. Again he heard that clear voice from behind, this time a little raised. The words failed to reach his brain, but the tone was one of cold and angry dissent, followed by an imperative order. Then once more his senses seemed to be leaving him. He passed into the world which seemed to consist only of himself and a youth in fisherman's oilskins, who was sometimes Furley, sometimes his own sister, sometimes the figure of a person who for the last twenty-four hours had been continually in his thoughts, who seemed at one moment to be sympathising with him and at another to be playing upon his face with a garden hose. Then it all faded away, and a sort of numbness crept over him. He made a desperate struggle for consciousness. There was something cold resting against his cheek. His fingers stole towards it. It was the flask, drawn from his own pocket and placed there by some unseen hand, the top already unscrewed, and the reviving odour stealing into his nostrils. He guided it to his lips with trembling fingers. A pleasant sense of warmth crept over him. His head fell back.

When he opened his eyes again, he first turned around for the tea by his bedside, then stared in front of him, wondering if these things which he saw were indeed displayed through an upraised blind. There was the marsh—a picture of still life—winding belts of sea creeping, serpent-like, away from him towards the land, with broad pools, in whose bosom, here and there, were flashes of a feeble sunlight. There were the clumps of wild lavender he had so often admired, the patches of deep meadow green, and, beating the air with their wings as they passed, came a flight of duck over his head. Very stiff and dazed, he staggered to his feet. There was the village to his right, red-tiled, familiar; the snug farmhouses, with their brown fields and belts of trees; the curve of the white road.

And then, with a single flash of memory, it all came back to him. He felt the top of his head, still sore; looked down at the stretch of shingle, empty now of any reminiscences; and finally, leaning heavily on his stick, he plodded back to the cottage, noticing, as he drew near, the absence of the motor-car from its place of shelter. Miles Furley was seated in his armchair, with a cup of tea in his hand and Mrs. West fussing over him, as Julian raised the latch and dragged himself into the sitting room. They both turned around at his entrance. Furley dropped his teaspoon and Mrs. West raised her hands above her head and shrieked. Julian sank into the nearest chair.

"Melodrama has come to me at last," he murmured. "Give me some tea—a whole teapotful, Mrs. West—and get a hot bath ready."

He waited until their temporary housekeeper had bustled out of the room. Then he concluded his sentence.

"I have been sandbagged," he announced impressively, and proceeded to relate the night's adventure to his host.

"This," declared Julian, about a couple of hours later, as he helped himself for the second time to bacon and eggs, "is a wonderful tribute to the soundness of our constitutions. Miles, it is evident that you and I have led righteous lives."

"Being sandbagged seems to have given you an appetite," Furley observed.

"And a game leg seems to have done the same for you," Julian rejoined. "Did the doctor ask you how you did it?"

Furley nodded.

"I just said that I slipped on the marshes. One doesn't talk of such little adventures as you and I experienced last night."

"By the bye, what does one do about them?" Julian enquired. "I feel a little dazed about it all, even now living in an unreal atmosphere and that sort of thing, you know. It seems to me that we ought to have out the bloodhounds and search for an engaging youth and a particularly disagreeable bully of a man, both dressed in brown oilskins and—"

"Oh, chuck it!" Furley intervened. "The intelligence department in charge of this bit of coast doesn't do things like that. What you want to remember, Julian, is to keep your mouth shut. I shall have a chap over to see me this afternoon, and I shall make a report to him."

"All the same," persisted Julian, "we—or rather I—was without a doubt a witness to an act of treason. By some subtle means connected with what seemed to be a piece of gas pipe, I have seen communication with the enemy established."

"You don't know that it was the enemy at all," Furley grunted.

"For us others," Julian replied, "there exists the post office, the telegraph office and the telephone. I decline to believe that any reasonable person would put out upon the sea in weather like last night's for the sake of delivering a letter to any harmless inhabitant of these regions. I will have my sensation, you see, Furley. I have suffered— thank heavens mine is a thick skull!—and I will not be cheated of my compensations."

"Well, keep your mouth shut, there's a good fellow, until after I have made my report to the Intelligence Officer," Furley begged. "He'll be here about four. You don't mind being about?"

"Not in the least," Julian promised. "So long as I am home for dinner, my people will be satisfied."

"I don't know how you'll amuse yourself this morning," Furley observed, "and I'm afraid I sha'n't be able to get out for the flighting this evening."

"Don't worry about me," Julian begged. "Remember that I am practically at home. It's only three miles to the Hall from here so you mustn't look upon me as an ordinary guest. I am going for a tramp in a few minutes."

"Lucky chap!" Furley declared enviously. "Sunshine like this makes one feel as though one were on the Riviera instead of in Norfolk. Shall you visit the scene of your adventure?"

"I may," Julian answered thoughtfully. "The instinct of the sleuthhound is beginning to stir in me. There is no telling how far it may lead."

Julian started on his tramp about half an hour later. He paused first at a bend in the road, about fifty yards down, and stepped up close to the hedge.

"The instinct of the sleuthhound," he said to himself, "is all very well, but why on earth haven't I told Furley about the car?"

He paused to consider the matter, conscious only of the fact that each time he had opened his lips to mention it, he had felt a marked but purposeless disinclination to do so. He consoled himself now with the reflection that the information would be more or less valueless until the afternoon, and he forthwith proceeded upon the investigation which he had planned out.

The road was still muddy, and the track of the tyres, which were of somewhat peculiar pattern, clearly visible. He followed it along the road for a matter of a mile and a half. Then he came to a standstill before a plain oak gate and was conscious of a distinct shock. On the top bar of the gate was painted in white letters.

MALTENBY HALL
TRADESMEN'S ENTRANCE

and it needed only the most cursory examination to establish the fact that the car whose track he had been following had turned in here. He held up his hand and stopped a luggage trolley which had just turned the bend in the avenue. The man pulled up and touched his hat.

"Where are you off to, Fellowes?" Julian enquired.

"I am going to Holt station, sir," the man replied, "after some luggage."

"Are there any guests at the Hall who motored here, do you know?" Julian asked.

"Only the young lady, sir," the man replied, "Miss Abbeway. She came in a little coupe Panhard."

Julian frowned thoughtfully.

"Has she been out in it this morning?" he asked.

The man shook his head.

"She broke down in it yesterday afternoon, sir," he answered, "about halfway up to the Hall here."

"Broke down?" Julian repeated. "Anything serious? Couldn't you put it right for her?"

"She wouldn't let me touch it, sir," the man explained. "She said she had two cracked sparking plugs, and she wanted to replace them herself. She has had some lessons, and I think she wanted a bit of practice."

"I see. Then the car is in the avenue now?"

"About half a mile up, on the left-hand side, sir, just by the big elm. Miss Abbeway said she was coming down this afternoon to put new plugs in."

"Then it's been there all the time since yesterday afternoon?" Julian persisted.

"The young lady wished it left there, sir. I could have put a couple of plugs in, in five minutes, and brought her up to the house, but she wouldn't hear of it."

"I see, Fellowes."

"Any luck with the geese last night, sir?" the man asked. "I heard there was a pack of them on Stiffkey Marshes."

"I got one. They came badly for us," Julian replied.

He made his way up the avenue. At exactly the spot indicated by the chauffeur a little coupe car was standing, drawn on to the turf. He glanced at the name of the maker and looked once more at the tracks upon the drive. Finally, he decided that his investigations were leading him in a most undesirable direction.

He turned back, walked across the marshes, where he found nothing to disturb him, and lunched with Furley, whose leg was now so much better that he was able to put it to the ground.

"What about this visitor of yours?" Julian asked, as they sat smoking afterwards. "I must be back at the Hall in time to dine to-night, you know. My people made rather a point of it."

Furley nodded.

"You'll be all right," he replied. "As a matter of fact, he isn't coming."

"Not coming?" Julian repeated. "Jove, I should have thought you'd have had intelligence officers by the dozen down here!"

"For some reason or other," Furley confided, "the affair has been handed over to the military authorities. I have had a man down to see me this morning, and he has taken full particulars. I don't know that they'll even worry you at all—until later on, at any rate."

"Jove, that seems queer!"

"Last night's happening was queer, for that matter," Furley continued. "Their only chance, I suppose, of getting to the bottom of it is to lie doggo as far as possible. It isn't like a police affair, you see. They don't want witnesses and a court of justice. One man's word and a rifle barrel does the trick."

Julian sighed.

"I suppose," he observed, "that if I do my duty as a loyal subject, I shall drop the curtain on last night. Seems a pity to have had an adventure like that and not be able to open one's mouth about it."

Furley grunted.

"You don't want to join the noble army of gas bags," he said. "Much better make up your mind that it was a dream."

"There are times," Julian confided, "when I am not quite sure that it wasn't."

III

Julian entered the drawing-room at Maltenby Hall a few minutes before dinner time that evening. His mother, who was alone and, for a wonder, resting, held out her hand for him to kiss and welcomed him with a charming smile. Notwithstanding her grey hair, she was still a remarkably young-looking woman, with a great reputation as a hostess.

"My dear Julian," she exclaimed, "you look like a ghost! Don't tell me that you had to sit up all night to shoot those wretched duck?"

Julian drew a chair to his mother's side and seated himself with a little air of relief.

"Never have I been more conscious of the inroads of age," he confided. "I can remember when, ten or fifteen years ago, I used to steal out of the house in the darkness and bicycle down to the marsh with a twenty-bore gun, on the chance of an odd shot."

"And I suppose," his mother went on, "after spending half the night wading about in the salt water, you spent the other half talking to that terrible Mr. Furley."

"Quite right. We got cold and wet through in the evening; we sat up talking till the small hours; we got cold and wet again this morning— and here I am."

"A converted sportsman," his mother observed. "I wish you could convert your friend, Mr. Furley. There's a perfectly terrible article of his in the National this month. I can't understand a word of it, but it reads like sheer anarchy."

"So long as the world exists," Julian remarked, "there must be Socialists, and Furley is at least honest."

"My dear Julian," his mother protested, "how can a Socialist be honest! Their attitude with regard to the war, too, is simply disgraceful. I am sure that in any other country that man Fenn, for instance, would be shot."

"What about your house party?" Julian enquired, with bland irrelevance.

"All arrived. I suppose they'll be down directly. Mr. Hannaway Wells is here."

"Good old Wells!" Julian murmured. "How does he look since he became a Cabinet Minister?"

"Portentous," Lady Maltenby replied; with a smile. "He doesn't look as though he would ever unbend. Then the Shervintons are here, and the Princess Torski—your friend Miss Abbeway's aunt."

"The Princess Torski?" Julian repeated. "Who on earth is she?"

"She was English," his mother explained, "a cousin of the Abbeways. She married in Russia and is on her way now to France to meet her husband, who is in command of a Russian battalion there. She seems quite a pleasant person, but not in the least like her niece."

"Miss Abbeway is still here, of course?"

"Naturally. I asked her for a week, and I think she means to stay. We talked for an hour after tea this afternoon, and I found her most interesting. She has been living in England for years, it seems, down in Chelsea, studying sculpture."

"She is a remarkably clever young woman," Julian said thoughtfully, "but a little incomprehensible. If the Princess Torski is her aunt, who were her parents?"

"Her father," the Countess replied, "was Colonel Richard Abbeway, who seems to have been military attache at St. Petersburg, years ago. He married a sister of the Princess Torski's husband, and from her this young woman inherited a title which she won't use and a large fortune. Colonel Abbeway was killed accidentally in the Russo-Japanese War, and her mother died a few years ago."

"No German blood, or anything of that sort, then?"

"My dear boy, what an idea!" his mother exclaimed reprovingly. "On the contrary, the Torskis are one of the most aristocratic families in Russia, and you know what the Abbeways are. The girl is excellently bred, and I think her charming in every way. Whatever made you suggest that she might have German blood in her?"

"No idea! Anyhow, I am glad she hasn't. Who else?"

"The Bishop," his mother continued, "looking very tired, poor dear! Doctor George Lennard, from Oxford, two young soldiers from Norwich, whom Charlie asked us to be civil to—and the great man himself."

"Tell me about the great man? I don't think I've seen him to speak to since he became Prime Minister."

"He declares that this is his first holiday this year. He is looking rather tired, but he has had an hour's shooting since he arrived, and seemed to enjoy it. Here's your father."

The Earl of Maltenby, who entered a moment later, was depressingly typical. He was as tall as his youngest son, with whom he shook hands absently and whom he resembled in no other way. He had the conventionally aristocratic features, thin lips and steely blue eyes. He was apparently a little annoyed.

"Anything wrong, dear?" Lady Maltenby asked.

Her husband took up his position on the hearthrug.

"I am annoyed with Stenson," he declared.

The Countess shook her head.

"It's too bad of you, Henry," she expostulated. "You've been trying to talk politics with him. You know that the poor man was only longing for forty-eight hours during which he could forget that he was Prime Minister of England."

"Precisely, my dear," Lord Maltenby agreed. "I can assure you that I have not transgressed in any way. A remark escaped me referring to the impossibility of providing beaters, nowadays, and to the fact that out of my seven keepers, five are fighting. I consider Mr. Stenson's comment was most improper, coming from one to whom the destinies of this country are confided."

"What did he say?" the Countess asked meekly.

"Something about wondering whether any man would be allowed to have seven keepers after the war," her husband replied, with an angry light in his eyes. "If a man like Stenson is going to encourage these socialistic ideas. I beg your pardon—the Bishop, my dear."

The remaining guests drifted in within the next few moments,— the Bishop, Julian's godfather, a curious blend of the fashionable and the devout, the anchorite and the man of the people; Lord and Lady Shervinton, elderly connections of the nondescript variety; Mr. Hannaway Wells, reserved yet, urbane, a wonderful type of the supreme success of mediocrity; a couple of young soldiers, light-hearted and out for a good time, of whom Julian took charge; an Oxford don, who had once been Lord Maltenby's tutor; and last of all the homely, very pleasant-looking, middle-aged lady, Princess Torski, followed by her niece. There were a few introductions still to be effected.

Whilst Lady Maltenby was engaged in this task, which she performed at all times with the unfailing tact of a great hostess, Julian broke off in his conversation with the two soldiers and looked steadfastly across the room at Catherine Abbeway, as though anxious to revise or complete his earlier impressions of her. She was of medium height, not unreasonably slim, with a deliberate but noticeably graceful carriage. Her complexion was inclined to be pale. She had large, soft brown eyes, and hair of an unusual shade of chestnut brown, arranged with remarkably effective simplicity. She wore a long string of green beads around her neck, a black tulle gown without any relief of colour, but a little daring in its cut. Her voice and laugh, as she stood talking to the Bishop, were delightful, and neither her gestures nor her accent betrayed the slightest trace of foreign blood. She was, without a doubt, extraordinarily attractive, gracious almost to freedom in her manner, and yet with that peculiar quality of aloofness only recognisable in the elect,—a very appreciable charm. Julian found his undoubted admiration only increased by his closer scrutiny. Nevertheless, as he watched her, there was a slightly puzzled frown upon his forehead, a sense of something like bewilderment mingled with those other feelings. His mother, who had turned to speak to the object of his attentions, beckoned him, and he crossed the room at once to their side.

"Julian is going to take you in to dinner, Miss Abbeway," the Countess announced, "and I hope you will be kind to him, for he's been out all night and a good part of the morning, too, shooting ducks and talking nonsense with a terrible Socialist."

Lady Maltenby passed on. Julian, leaning on his stick, looked down with a new interest into the face which had seldom been out of his thoughts since their first meeting, a few weeks ago.

"Tell me, Mr. Orden," she asked, "which did you find the more exhausting—tramping the marshes for sport, or discussing sociology with your friend?"

"As a matter of fact," he replied, "we didn't tramp the marshes. We stood still and got uncommonly wet. And I shot a goose, which made me very happy."

"Then it must have been the conversation," she declared. "Is your friend a prophet or only one of the multitude?"

"A prophet, most decidedly. He is a Mr. Miles Furley, of whom you must have heard."

She started a little.

"Miles Furley!" she repeated. "I had no idea that he lived in this part of the world."

"He has a small country house somewhere in Norfolk," Julian told her, "and he takes a cottage down here at odd times for the wild-fowl shooting."

"Will you take me to see him to-morrow?" she asked.

"With pleasure, so long as you promise not to talk socialism with him."

"I will promise that readily, out of consideration to my escort. I wonder how it is," she went on, looking up at him a little thoughtfully, "that you dislike serious subjects so much."

"A frivolous turn of mind, I suppose," he replied. "I certainly prefer to talk art with you."

"But nowadays," she protested, "it is altogether the fashion down at Chelsea to discard art and talk politics."

"It's a fashion I shouldn't follow," he advised. "I should stick to art, if I were you."

"Well, that depends upon how you define politics, of course. I don't mean Party politics. I mean the science of living, as a whole, not as a unit."

The Princess ambled up to them.

"I don't know what your political views are, Mr. Orden," she said, "but you must look out for shocks if you discuss social questions with my niece. In the old days they would never have allowed her to live in Russia. Even now, I consider some of her doctrines the most pernicious I ever heard."

"Isn't that terrible from an affectionate aunt!"

Catherine laughed, as the Princess passed on. "Tell me some more about your adventures last night?"

She looked up into his face, and Julian was suddenly conscious from whence had come that faint sense of mysterious trouble which had been with him during the last few minutes. The slight quiver of her lips brought it all back to him. Her mouth, beyond a doubt, with its half tender, half mocking curve, was the mouth which he had seen in that tangled dream of his, when he had lain fighting for consciousness upon the marshes.

IV

Julian, absorbed for the first few minutes of dinner by the crystallisation of this new idea which had now taken a definite place in his brain, found his conversational powers somewhat at a discount. Catherine very soon, however, asserted her claim upon his attention.

"Please do your duty and tell me about things," she begged. "Remember that I am Cinderella from Bohemia, and I scarcely know a soul here."

"Well, there aren't many to find out about, are there?" he replied. "Of course you know Stenson?"

"I have been gazing at him with dilated eyes," she confided. "Is that not the proper thing to do? He seems to me very ordinary and very hungry."

"Well, then, there is the Bishop."

"I knew him at once from his photographs. He must spend the whole of the time when he isn't in church visiting the photographer. However, I like him. He is talking to my aunt quite amiably. Nothing does aunt so much good as to sit next a bishop."

"The Shervintons you know all about, don't you?" he went on. "The soldiers are just young men from the Norwich barracks, Doctor Lennard was my father's tutor at Oxford, and Mr. Hannaway Wells is our latest Cabinet Minister."

"He still has the novice's smirk," she remarked. "A moment ago I heard him tell his neighbour that he preferred not to discuss the war. He probably thinks that there is a spy under the table."

"Well, there we are—such as we are," Julian concluded. "There is no one left except me."

"Then tell me all about yourself," she suggested. "Really, when I come to think of it, considering the length of our conversations, you have been remarkably reticent. You are the youngest of the family, are you not? How many brothers are there?"

"There were four," he told her. "Henry was killed at Ypres last year. Guy is out there still. Richard is a Brigadier."

"And you?"

"I am a barrister by profession, but I went out with the first Inns of Court lot for a little amateur soldiering and lost part of my foot at Mons. Since then I have been indulging in the unremunerative and highly monotonous occupation of censoring."

"Monotonous indeed, I should imagine," she agreed. "You spend your time reading other people's letters, do you not, just to be sure that there are no communications from the enemy?"

"Precisely," he assented. "We discover ciphers and all sorts of things."

"What brainy people you must be!"

"We are, most of us."

"Do you do anything else?"

"Well, I've given up censoring for the present," he confided. "I am going back to my profession."

"As a barrister?"

"Just so. I might add that I do a little hack journalism."

"How modest!" she murmured. "I suppose you write the leading articles for the Times!"

"For a very young lady," Julian observed impressively, "you have marvellous insight. How did you guess my secret?"

"I am better at guessing secrets than you are," she retorted a little insolently.

He was silent for some moments. The faint curve of her lips had again given him almost a shock.

"Have you a brother?" he asked abruptly.

"No. Why?"

"Because I met some one quite lately—within the last few hours, as a matter of fact—with a mouth exactly like yours."

"But what a horrible thing!" she exclaimed, drawing out a little mirror from the bag by her side and gazing into it. "How unpleasant to have any one else going about with a mouth exactly like one's own! No, I never had a brother, Mr. Orden, or a sister, and, as you may have heard, I am an enfant mechante. I live in London, I model very well, and I talk very bad sociology. As I think I told you, I know your anarchist friend, Miles Furley."

"I shouldn't call Furley an anarchist," protested Julian.

"Well, he is a Socialist. I admit that we are rather lax in our definitions. You see, there is just one subject, of late years, which has brought together the Socialists and the Labour men, the Syndicalists and the Communists, the Nationalists and the Internationalists. All those who work for freedom are learning breadth. If they ever find a leader, I think that this dear, smug country of yours may have to face the greatest surprise of its existence."

Julian looked at her curiously.

"You have ideas, Miss Abbeway."

"So unusual in a woman!" she mocked. "Do you notice how every one is trying to avoid the subject of the war? I give them another half-course, don't you? I am sure they cannot keep it up."

"They won't go the distance," Julian whispered. "Listen."

"The question to be considered," Lord Shervinton pronounced, "is not so much when the war will be over as what there is to stop it? That is a point which I think we can discuss without inviting official indiscretions."

"If other means fail," declared the Bishop, "Christianity will stop it. The conscience of the world is already being stirred."

"Our enemies," the Earl pronounced confidently from his place at the head of the table, "are already a broken race. They are on the point of exhaustion. Austria is, if possible, in a worse plight. That is what will end the war—the exhaustion of our opponents."

"The deciding factor," Mr. Hannaway Wells put in, with a very non-committal air, "will probably be America. She will bring her full strength into the struggle just at the crucial moment. She will probably do what we farther north have as yet failed to do: she will pierce the line and place the German armies in Flanders in peril."

The Cabinet Minister's views were popular. There was a little murmur of approval, something which sounded almost like a purr of content. It was just one more expression of that strangely discreditable yet almost universal failing,—the over-reliance upon others. The quiet remark of the man who suddenly saw fit to join in the discussion struck a chilling and a disturbing note.

"There is one thing which could end the war at any moment," Mr. Stenson said, leaning a little forward, "and that is the will of the people."

There was perplexity as well as discomfiture in the minds of his hearers.

"The people?" Lord Shervinton repeated. "But surely the people speak through the mouths of their rulers?"

"They have been content to, up to the present," the Prime Minister agreed, "but Europe may still see strange and dramatic events before many years are out."

"Do go on, please," the Countess begged.

Mr. Stenson shook his head.

"Even as a private individual I have said more than I intended," he replied. "I have only one thing to say about the war in public, and that is that we

E. PHILLIPS OPPENHEIM

are winning, that we must win, that our national existence depends upon winning, and that we shall go on until we do win. The obstacles between us and victory, which may remain in our minds, are not to be spoken of."

There was a brief and somewhat uncomfortable pause. It was understood that the subject was to be abandoned. Julian addressed a question to the Bishop across the table. Lord Maltenby consulted Doctor Lennard as to the date of the first Punic War. Mr. Stenson admired the flowers. Catherine, who had been sitting with her eyes riveted upon the Prime Minister, turned to her neighbour.

"Tell me about your amateur journalism, Mr. Orden?" she begged. "I have an idea that it ought to be interesting."

"Deadly dull, I can assure you."

"You write about politics? Or perhaps you are an art critic? I ought to be on my best behaviour, in case."

"I know little about art," he assured her. "My chief interest in life—outside my profession, of course—lies in sociology."

His little confession had been impulsive. She raised her eyebrows.

"You are in earnest, I believe!" she exclaimed. "Have I really found an Englishman who is in earnest?"

"I plead guilty. It is incorrect philosophy but a distinct stimulus to life."

"What a pity," she sighed, "that you are so handicapped by birth! Sociology cannot mean anything very serious for you. Your perspective is naturally distorted."

"What about yourself?" he asked pertinently.

"The vanity of us women!" she murmured. "I have grown to look upon myself as being an exception. I forget that there might be others. You might even be one of our prophets—a Paul Fiske in disguise."

His eyes narrowed a little as he looked at her closely. From across the table, the Bishop broke off an interesting discussion on the subject of his addresses to the working classes, and the Earl set down his wineglass with an impatient gesture.

"Does no one really know," Mr. Stenson asked, "who Paul Fiske is?"

"No one, sir," Mr. Hannaway Wells replied. "I thought it wise, a short time ago, to set on foot the most searching enquiries, but they were absolutely fruitless."

The Bishop coughed.

"I must plead guilty," he confessed, "to having visited the offices of The Monthly Review with the same object. I left a note for him there, in charge of the editor, inviting him to a conference at my house. I received no reply. His anonymity seems to be impregnable."

"Whoever he may be," the Earl declared, "he ought to be muzzled. He is a traitor to his country."

"I cannot agree with you, Lord Maltenby," the Bishop said firmly. "The very danger of the man's doctrines lies in their clarity of thought, their extraordinary proximity to the fundamental truths of life."

"The man is, at any rate," Doctor Lennard interposed, "the most brilliant anonymous writer since the days of Swift and the letters of Junius."

Mr. Stenson for a moment hesitated. He seemed uncertain whether or no to join in the conversation. Finally, impulse swayed him.

"Let us all be thankful," he said, "that Paul Fiske is content with the written word. If the democracy of England found themselves to-day with such a leader, it is he who would be ruling the country, and not I."

"The man is a pacifist!" the Earl protested.

"So we all are," the Bishop declared warmly. "We are all pacifists in the sense that we are lovers of peace. There is not one of us who does not deplore the horrors of to-day. There is not one of us who is not passionately seeking for the master mind which can lead us out of it."

"There is only one way out," the Earl insisted, "and that is to beat the enemy."

"It is the only obvious way," Julian intervened, joining in the conversation for the first time, "but meanwhile, with every tick of the clock a fellow creature dies."

"It is a question," Mr. Hannaway Wells reflected, "whether the present generation is not inclined to be mawkish with regard to human life. History has shown us the marvellous benefits which have accrued to the greatest nations through the lessening of population by means of warfare."

"History has also shown us," Doctor Lennard observed, "that the last resource of force is force. No brain has ever yet devised a logical scheme for international arbitration."

"Human nature, I am afraid, has changed extraordinarily little since the days of the Philistines," the Bishop confessed.

Julian turned to his companion.

"Well, they've all settled it amongst themselves, haven't they?" he murmured. "Here you may sit and listen to what may be called the modern voice."

"Yet there is one thing wanting," she whispered. "What do you suppose, if he were here at this moment, Paul Fiske would say? Do you think that he would be content to listen to these brazen voices and accept their verdict?"

"Without irreverence," Julian answered, "or comparison, would Jesus Christ?"

"With the same proviso," she retorted, "I might reply that Jesus Christ, from all we know of him, might reign wonderfully in the Kingdom of Heaven, but he certainly wouldn't be able to keep together a Cabinet in Downing Street! Still, I am beginning to believe in your sincerity. Do you think that Paul Fiske is sincere?"

"I believe," Julian replied, "that he sees the truth and struggles to express it."

The women were leaving the table. She leaned towards him.

"Please do not be long," she whispered. "You must admit that I have been an admirable dinner companion. I have talked to you all the time on your own subject. You must come and talk to me presently about art."

Julian, with his hand on the back of his chair, watched the women pass out of the soft halo of the electric lights into the gloomier shadows of the high, vaulted room, Catherine a little slimmer than most of the others, and with a strange grace of slow movement which must have come to her from some Russian ancestor. Her last words lingered in his mind. He was to talk to her about art! A fleeting vision of the youth in the yellow oilskins mocked him. He remembered his morning's tramp and the broken-down motor-car under the trees. The significance of these things was beginning to take shape in his mind. He resumed his seat, a little dazed.

V

Maltenby was one of those old-fashioned houses where the port is served as a lay sacrament and the call of the drawing-room is responded to tardily. After the departure of the women, Doctor Lennard drew his chair up to Julian's.

"An interesting face, your dinner companion's," he remarked. "They tell me that she is a very brilliant young lady."

"She certainly has gifts," acknowledged Julian.

"I watched her whilst she was talking to you," the Oxford don continued. "She is one of those rare young women whose undoubted beauty is put into the background by their general attractiveness. Lady Maltenby was telling me fragments of her history. It appears that she is thinking of giving up her artistic career for some sort of sociological work."

"It is curious," Julian reflected, "how the cause of the people has always appealed to gifted Russians. England, for instance, produces no real democrats of genius. Russia seems to claim a monopoly of them."

"There is nothing so stimulating as a sense of injustice for bringing the best out of a man or woman," Doctor Lennard pointed out. "Russia, of course, for many years has been shamefully misgoverned."

The conversation, owing to the intervention of other of the guests, became general and platitudinal. Soon after, Mr. Stenson rose and excused himself. His secretary, who had been at the telephone, desired a short conference. There was a brief silence after his departure.

"Stenson," the Oxonian observed, "is beginning to show signs of strain."

"Why not?" Lord Shervinton pointed out. "He came into office full of the most wonderful enthusiasm. His speeches rang through the world like a clarion note. He converted waverers. He lit fires which still burn. But he is a man of movement. This present stagnation is terribly irksome to him. I heard him speak last week, and I was disappointed. He seems to have lost his inspiration. What he needs is a stimulus of some sort, even of disaster."

"I wonder," the Bishop reflected, "if he is really afraid of the people?"

"I consider his remark concerning them most ill-advised," Lord Maltenby declared pompously.

"I know the people," the Bishop continued, "and I love them. I think, too, that they trust me. Yet I am not sure that I cannot see a glimmering of what is at the back of Stenson's mind. There are a good many millions in the country who honestly believe that war is primarily an affair of the politicians; who believe, too, that victory means a great deal more to what they term 'the upper classes' than it does to them. Yet, in every sense of the word, they are bearing an equal portion of the fight, because, when it comes down to human life, the life of the farm labourer's son is of the same intrinsic value as the life of the peer's."

Lord Maltenby moved a little in his chair. There was a slight frown upon his aristocratic forehead. He disagreed entirely with the speaker, with whom he feared, however, to cross swords. Mr. Hannaway Wells, who had been waiting for his opportunity, took charge of the conversation. He spoke in a reserved manner, his fingers playing with the stem of his wineglass.

"I must confess," he said, "that I feel the deepest interest in what the Bishop has just said. I could not talk to you about the military situation, even if I knew more than you do, which is not the case, but I think it is clear that we have reached something like a temporary impasse. There certainly seems to be no cause for alarm upon any front, yet, not only in London, but in Paris and even Rome, there is a curious uneasiness afoot, for which no one can account which no one can bring home to any definite cause. In the same connection, we have confidential information that a new spirit of hopefulness is abroad in Germany. It has been reported to us that sober, clear-thinking men—and there are a few of them, even in Germany—have predicted peace before a month is out."

"The assumption is," Doctor Lennard interpolated, "that Germany has something up her sleeve."

"That is not only the assumption," the Cabinet Minister replied, "but it is also, I believe, the truth."

"One could apprehend and fear a great possible danger," Lord Shervinton observed, "if the Labour Party in Germany were as strong as ours, or if our own Labour Party were entirely united. The present conditions, however, seem to me to give no cause for alarm."

"That is where I think you are wrong," Hannaway Wells declared. "If the Labour Party in Germany were as strong as ours, they would be strong enough to overthrow the Hohenzollern clique, to stamp out the militarism against which we are at war, to lay the foundations of a great German republic with whom we could make the sort of peace for which every Englishman hopes. The danger, the real danger which we have to face, would lie in an amalgamation of the Labour Party, the Socialists and the Syndicalists in this country, and in their insisting upon treating with the weak Labour Party in Germany."

"I agree with the Bishop," Julian pronounced. "The unclassified democracy of our country may believe itself hardly treated, but individually it is intensely patriotic. I do not believe that its leaders would force the hand of the country towards peace, unless they received full assurance that their confreres in Germany were able to assume a dominant place in the government of that country—a place at least equal to the influence of the democracy here."

Doctor Lennard glanced at the speaker a little curiously. He had known Julian since he was a boy but had never regarded him as anything but a dilettante.

"You may not know it," he said, "but you are practically expounding the views of that extraordinary writer of whom we were speaking—Paul Fiske."

"I have been told," the Bishop remarked, cracking a walnut, "that Paul Fiske is the pseudonym of a Cabinet Minister."

"And I," Hannaway Wells retorted, "have been informed most credibly that he is a Church of England clergyman."

"The last rumour I heard," Lord Shervinton put in, "was that he is a grocer in a small way of business at Wigan."

"Dear me!" Doctor Lennard remarked. "The gossips have covered enough ground! A man at a Bohemian club of which I am a member—the Savage Club, in fact—assured me that he was an opium drugged journalist, kept alive by the charity of a few friends; a human wreck, who was once the editor of an important London paper."

"You have some slight connection with journalism, have you not, Julian?" the Earl asked his son condescendingly. "Have you heard no reports?"

"Many," Julian replied, "but none which I have been disposed to credit. I should imagine, myself, that Paul Fiske is a man who believes, having created a public, that his written words find an added value from the fact that he obviously desires neither reward nor recognition; just in the same way as the really earnest democrats of twenty years ago scoffed at the idea of a seat in Parliament, or of breaking bread in any way with the enemy."

"It was a fine spirit, that," the Bishop declared. "I am not sure that we are not all of us a little over-inclined towards compromises. The sapping away of conscience is so easy."

The dining-room door was thrown open, and the butler announced a visitor.

"Colonel Henderson, your lordship."

They all turned around in their places. The colonel, a fine, military-looking figure of a man, shook hands with Lord Maltenby.

"My most profound apologies, sir," he said, as he accepted a chair. "The Countess was kind enough to say that if I were not able to get away in time for dinner, I might come up afterwards."

"You are sure that you have dined?"

"I had something at Mess, thank you."

"A glass of port, then?"

The Colonel helped himself from the decanter which was passed towards him and exchanged greetings with several of the guests to whom his host introduced him.

"No raids or invasions, I hope, Colonel?" the latter asked.

"Nothing quite so serious as that, I am glad to say. We have had a little excitement of another sort, though. One of my men caught a spy this morning."

Every one was interested. Even after three years of war, there was still something fascinating about the word.

"Dear me!" Lord Maltenby exclaimed. "I should scarcely have considered our out-of-the-way part of the world sufficiently important to attract attentions of that sort."

"It was a matter of communication," the Colonel confided. "There was an enemy submarine off here last night, and we have reason to believe that a message was landed. We caught one fellow just at dawn."

"What did you do with him?" the Bishop asked.

"We shot him an hour ago," was the cool reply.

"Are there any others at large?" Julian enquired, leaning forward.

"One other," the Colonel acknowledged, sipping his wine appreciatively. "My military police here, however, are very intelligent, and I should think it very doubtful whether he can escape."

"Was the man who was shot a foreigner?" the Earl asked. "I trust that he was not one of my tenants?"

"He was a stranger," was the prompt assurance.

"And his companion?" Julian ventured.

"His companion is believed to have been quite a youth. There is a suggestion that he escaped in a motor-car, but he is probably hiding in the neighbourhood."

Lord Maltenby frowned. There seemed to him something incongruous in the fact that a deed of this sort should have been committed in his domain without his knowledge. He rose to his feet.

"The Countess is probably relying upon some of us for bridge," he said. "I hope, Colonel, that you will take a hand."

The men rose and filed slowly out of the room. The Colonel, however, detained his host, and Julian also lingered.

"I hope, Lord Maltenby," the former said, "that you will excuse my men, but they tell me that they find it necessary to search your garage for a car which has been seen in the neighbourhood."

"Search my garage?" Lord Maltenby repeated, frowning.

"There is no doubt," the Colonel explained, "that a car was made use of last night by the man who is still at large, and it is very possible that it was stolen. You will understand, I am sure, that any enquiries which my men may feel it their duty to make are actuated entirely by military necessity."

"Quite so," the Earl acceded, still a little puzzled. "You will find my head chauffeur a most responsible man. He will, I am sure, give them every possible information. So far as I am aware, however, there is no strange car in the garage. Do you know of any, Julian?"

"Only Miss Abbeway's," his son replied. "Her little Panhard was out in the avenue all night, waiting for her to put some plugs in. Every one else seems to have come by train."

The Colonel raised his eyebrows very slightly and moved slowly towards the door.

"The matter is in the hands of my police," he said, "but if you could excuse me for half a moment, Lord Maltenby, I should like to speak to your head chauffeur."

"By all means," the Earl replied. "I will take you round to the garage myself."

VI

Julian entered the drawing-room hurriedly a few minutes later. He glanced around quickly, conscious of a distinct feeling of disappointment. His mother, who was arranging a bridge table, called him over to her side.

"You have the air, my dear boy, of missing some one," she remarked with a smile.

"I want particularly to speak to Miss Abbeway," he confided.

Lady Maltenby smiled tolerantly.

"After nearly two hours of conversation at dinner! Well, I won't keep you in suspense. She wanted a quiet place to write some letters, so I sent her into the boudoir."

Julian hastened off, with a word of thanks. The boudoir was a small room opening from the suite which had been given to the Princess and her niece a quaint, almost circular apartment, hung with faded blue Chinese silk and furnished with fragments of the Louis Seize period,—a rosewood cabinet, in particular, which had come from Versailles, and which was always associated in Julian's mind with the faint fragrance of two Sevres jars of dried rose leaves. The door opened almost noiselessly.

Catherine, who was seated before a small, ebony writing table, turned her head at his entrance.

"You?" she exclaimed.

Julian listened for a moment and then closed the door. She sat watching him, with the pen still in her fingers.

"Miss Abbeway," he said, "have you heard any news this evening?"

The pen with which she had been tapping the table was suddenly motionless. She turned a little farther around.

"News?" she repeated. "No! Is there any?"

"A man was caught upon the marshes this morning and shot an hour ago. They say that he was a spy."

She sat as though turned to stone.

"Well?"

"The military police are still hunting for his companion. They are now searching the garage here to see if they can find a small, grey, coupe car."

This time she remained speechless, but all those ill-defined fears which had gathered in his heart seemed suddenly to come to a head.

Her appearance had changed curiously during the last hour. There was a hunted, almost a desperate gleam in her eyes, a drawn look about her mouth as she sat looking at him.

"How do you know this?" she asked.

"The Colonel of the regiment stationed here has just arrived. He is down in the garage now with my father."

"Shot!" she murmured. "Most Dieu!"

"I want to help you," he continued.

Her eyes questioned him almost fiercely.

"You are sure?"

"I am sure."

"You know what it means?"

"I do."

"How did you guess the truth?"

"I remembered your mouth," he told her. "I saw your car last night, and I traced it up the avenue this morning."

"A mouth isn't much to go by," she observed, with a very wan smile.

"It happens to be your mouth," he replied.

She rose to her feet and stood for a moment as though listening. Then she thrust her hand down into the bosom of her gown and produced a small roll of paper wrapped in a sheet of oilskin. He took it from her at once and slipped it into the breast pocket of his coat.

"You understand what you are doing?" she persisted.

"Perfectly;" he replied.

She crossed the room towards the hearthrug and stood there for a moment, leaning against the mantelpiece.

"Is there anything else I can do?" he asked.

She turned around. There was a wonderful change in her face.

"No one saw me," she said. "I do not think that there is any one but you who could positively identify the car. Neither my aunt nor the maid who is with us has any idea that I left my room last night."

"Your clothes?"

"Absolutely destroyed," she assured him with a smile. "Some day I hope I'll find courage to ask you whether you thought them becoming."

"Some day," he retorted, a little grimly, "I am going to have a very serious talk with you, Miss Abbeway."

"Shall you be very stern?"

He made no response to her lighter mood. The appeal in her eyes left him colder than ever.

"I wish to save your life," he declared, "and I mean to do it. At the same time, I cannot forget your crime or my complicity in it."

"If you feel like that, then," she said a little defiantly, "tell the truth. I knew the risk I was running. I am not afraid, even now. You can give me back those papers, if you like. I can assure you that the person on whom they are found will undoubtedly be shot."

"Then I shall certainly retain possession of them," he decided.

"You are very chivalrous, sir," she ventured, smiling.

"I happen to be only selfish," Julian replied. "I even despise myself for what I am doing. I am turning traitor myself, simply because I could not bear the thought of what might happen to you if you were discovered."

"You like me, then, a little, Mr. Orden?" she asked.

"Twenty-four hours ago," he sighed, "I had hoped to answer that question before it was asked."

"This is very tantalising," she murmured. "You are going to save my life, then, and afterwards treat me as though I were a leper?"

"I shall hope," he said, "that you may have explanations—that I may find—"

She held out her hand and stopped him. Once more, for a moment, her eyes were distended, her form was tense. She was listening intently.

"There is some one coming," she whispered—"two or three men, I think. What fools we have been! We ought to have decided—about the car."

Her teeth came together for a moment. It was her supreme effort at self-control. Then she laughed almost naturally, lit a cigarette, and seated herself upon the arm of an easy-chair.

"You are interfering shockingly with my correspondence," she declared, "and I am sure that they want you for bridge. Here comes Lord Maltenby to tell you so," she added, glancing towards the door.

Lord Maltenby was very pompous, very stiff, and yet apologetic. He considered the whole affair in which he had become involved ridiculous.

"Miss Abbeway," he said, "I beg to present to you Colonel Henderson. An unfortunate occurrence took place here last night, which it has become the duty of—er—Colonel Henderson to clear up. He wishes to ask you a question concerning—er—a motor-car."

Colonel Henderson frowned. He stepped a little forward with the air of wishing to exclude the Earl from further speech.

"May I ask, Miss Abbeway," he began, "whether the small coupe car, standing about a hundred yards down the back avenue, is yours?"

"It is," she assented, with a little sigh. "It won't go."

"It won't go?" the Colonel repeated.

"I thought you might know something about cars," she explained. "They tell me that two of the sparking plugs are cracked. I am thinking of replacing them tomorrow morning, if I can get Mr. Orden to help me."

"How long has the car been there in its present condition, then?" the Colonel enquired.

"Since about five o'clock yesterday afternoon," she replied.

"You don't think it possible that it could have been out on the road anywhere last night, then?"

"Out on the road!" she laughed. "Why, I couldn't get it up to the garage! You go and look at it, Colonel, if you understand cars. Fellowes, the chauffeur here, had a look at the plugs when I brought it in, and you'll find that they haven't been touched."

"I trust," the Earl intervened, "that my chauffeur offered to do what was necessary?"

"Certainly he did, Lord Maltenby," she assured him. "I am trying hard to be my own mechanic, though, and I have set my mind on changing those plugs myself to-morrow morning."

"You are your own chauffeur, then, Miss Abbeway?" her inquisitor asked.

"Absolutely."

"You can change a wheel, perhaps?"

"Theoretically I can, but as a matter of fact I have never had to do it.'"

"Your tyres," Colonel Henderson continued, "are of somewhat unusual pattern."

"They are Russian," she told him. "I bought them for that reason. As a matter of fact, they are very good tyres."

"Miss Abbeway," the Colonel said, "I don't know whether you are aware that my police are in search of a spy who is reported to have escaped from the marshes last night in a small motor-car which was left at a certain spot in the Salthouse road. I do not believe that there are two tyres such as yours in Norfolk. How do you account for their imprint being clearly visible along the road to a certain spot near Salthouse? My police have taken tracings of them this morning."

Catherine remained perfectly speechless. A slow smile of triumph dawned upon her accuser's lips. Lord Maltenby's eyebrows were upraised as though in horror.

"Perhaps," Julian interposed, "I can explain the tyre marks upon the road. Miss Abbeway drove me down to Furley's cottage, where I spent the night, late in the afternoon. The marks were still there when I returned this morning, because I noticed them."

"The same marks?" the Colonel asked, frowning.

"Without a doubt the same marks," Julian replied. "In one place, where we skidded a little, I recognized them."

Colonel Henderson smiled a little more naturally.

"I begin to have hopes," he acknowledged frankly, "that I have been drawn into another mare's nest. Nevertheless, I am bound to ask you this question, Miss Abbeway. Did you leave your room at all during last night?"

"Not unless I walked in my sleep," she answered, "but you had better make enquiries of my aunt, and Parkins, our maid. They sleep one on either side of me."

"You would not object," the Colonel continued, more cheerfully still, "if my people thought well to have your things searched?"

"Not in the least," Catherine replied coolly, "only if you unpack my trunks, I beg that you will allow my maid to fold and unfold my clothes."

"I do not think," Colonel Henderson said to Lord Maltenby, "that I have any more questions to ask Miss Abbeway at present."

"In which case we will return to the drawing-room," the Earl suggested a little stiffly. "Miss Abbeway, you will, I trust, accept my apologies for our intrusion upon you. I regret that any guest of mine should have been subjected to a suspicion so outrageous."

Catherine laughed softly.

"Not outrageous really, dear Lord Maltenby," she said. "I do not quite know of what I have been suspected, but I am sure Colonel Henderson would not have asked me these questions if it had not been his duty."

"If you had not been a guest in this house, Miss Abbeway," the Colonel assured her, with some dignity, "I should have had you arrested first and questioned afterwards."

"You come of a race of men, Colonel Henderson, who win wars," she declared graciously. "You know your own mind."

"You will be joining us presently, I hope?" Lord Maltenby enquired from the door.

"In a very few minutes," she promised.

The door closed behind them. Catherine waited for a moment, then she sank a little hysterically into a chair.

"I cannot avoid a touch of melodrama, you see," she confessed. "It goes with my character and nationality. But seriously, now that that is over, I do not consider myself in the slightest danger. The poor fellow who was shot this morning belongs to a different order of people. He has been a spy over here since the beginning of the war."

"And what are you?" he asked bluntly.

She laughed up in his face.

"A quite attractive young woman," she declared,—"at least I feel sure you will think so when you know me better."

VII

I t was about half-past ten on the following morning when Julian, obeying a stentorian invitation to enter, walked into Miles Furley's sitting room. Furley was stretched upon the couch, smoking a pipe and reading the paper.

"Good man!" was his hearty greeting. "I hoped you'd look me up this morning."

Julian dragged up the other dilapidated-looking easy-chair to the log fire and commenced to fill his pipe from the open jar.

"How's the leg?" he enquired.

"Pretty nearly all right again," Furley answered cheerfully. "Seems to me I was frightened before I was hurt. What about your head?"

"No inconvenience at all," Julian declared, stretching himself out. "I suppose I must have a pretty tough skull."

"Any news?"

"News enough, of a sort, if you haven't heard it. They caught the man who sandbagged me, and who I presume sawed your plank through, and shot him last night."

"The devil they did!" Furley exclaimed, taking his pipe from his mouth. "Shot him? Who the mischief was he, then?"

"It appears," Julian replied, "that he was a German hairdresser, who escaped from an internment camp two years ago and has been at large ever since, keeping in touch, somehow or other, with his friends on the other side. He must have known the game was up as soon as he was caught. He didn't even attempt any defence."

"Shot, eh?" Furley repeated, relighting his pipe. "Serves him damned well right!"

"You think so, do you?" Julian remarked pensively.

"Who wouldn't? I hate espionage. So does every Englishman. That's why we are such duffers at the game, I suppose."

Julian watched his friend with a slight frown.

"How in thunder did you get mixed up with this affair, Furley?" he asked quietly.

Furley's bewilderment was too natural to be assumed. He removed his pipe from his teeth and stared at his friend.

"What the devil are you driving at, Julian?" he demanded. "I can assure you that I went out, the night before last, simply to make one of the rounds which falls to my lot when I am in this part of the world and nominated for duty. There are eleven of us between here and Sheringham, special constables of a humble branch of the secret service, if you like to put it so. We are a well-known institution amongst the initiated. I've plodded these marshes sometimes from midnight till daybreak, and although one's always hearing rumours, until last night I have never seen or heard of a single unusual incident."

"You had no idea, then," Julian persisted, "what it was that you were on the look-out for the night before last? You had no idea, say, from any source whatever, that there was going to be an attempt on the part of the enemy to communicate with friends on this side?"

"Good God, no! Even to have known it would have been treason."

"You admit that?"

Furley drew himself stiffly up in his chair. His mass of brown hair seemed more unkempt than usual, his hard face sterner than ever by reason of its disfiguring frown.

"What the hell do you mean, Julian?"

"I mean," Julian replied, "that I have reason to suspect you, Furley, of holding or attempting to hold secret communication with an enemy country."

The pipestem which he was holding snapped in Furley's fingers. His eyes were filled with fury.

"Damn you, Julian!" he exclaimed. "If I could stand on two legs, I'd break your head. How dare you come here and talk such rubbish."

"Isn't there some truth in what I have just said?" Julian asked sternly.

"Not a word."

Julian was silent for a moment. Furley was sitting upright upon the sofa, his keen eyes aglint with anger.

"I am waiting for an explanation, Julian," he announced.

"You shall have it," was the prompt reply. "The companion of the man who was shot, for whom the police are searching at this moment, is a guest in my father's house. I have had to go to the extent of lying to save her from detection."

"Her?" Furley gasped.

"Yes! The youth in fisherman's oilskins, into whose hands that message passed last night, is Miss Catherine Abbeway. The young lady has referred me to you for some explanation as to its being in her possession."

Furley remained absolutely speechless for several moments. His first expression was one of dazed bewilderment. Then the light broke in upon him. He began to understand. When he spoke, all the vigour had left his tone.

"You'll have to let me think about this for a moment, Julian," he said.

"Take your own time. I only want an explanation."

Furley recovered himself slowly. He stretched out his hand towards the pipe rack, filled another pipe and lit it. Then he began.

"Julian," he said, "every word that I have spoken to you about the night before last is the truth. There is a further confession, however, which under the circumstances I have to make. I belong to a body of men who are in touch with a similar association in Germany, but I have no share in any of the practical doings—the machinery, I might call it—of our organisation. I have known that communications have passed back and forth, but I imagined that this was done through neutral countries. I went out the night before last as an ordinary British citizen, to do my duty. I had not the faintest idea that there was to be any attempt to land a communication here, referring to the matters in which I am interested. I should imagine that the proof, of my words lies in the fact that efforts were made to prevent my reaching my beat, and that you, my substitute, whom I deliberately sent to take my place, were attacked."

"I accept your word so far," Julian said. "Please go on."

"I am an Englishman and a patriot," Furley continued, "just as much as you are, although you are a son of the Earl of Maltenby, and you fought in the war. You must listen to me without prejudice. There are thoughtful men in England, patriots to the backbone, trying to grope their way to the truth about this bloody sacrifice. There are thoughtful men in Germany on the same tack. If, for the betterment of the world, we should seek to come into touch with one another, I do not consider that treason, or communicating with an enemy country in the ordinary sense of the word."

"I see," Julian muttered. "What you are prepared to plead guilty to is holding communication with members of the Labour and Socialist Party in Germany."

"I plead guilty to nothing," Furley answered, with a touch of his old fierceness. "Don't talk like your father and his class, Julian. Get away from it. Be yourself. Your Ministers can't end the war. Your Government can't. They opened their mouth too wide at first. They made too many commitments. Ask Stenson. He'll tell you that I'm speaking the truth. So it goes on, and day by day it costs the world a few hundred or a few thousand human lives, and God knows how much of man's labour and brains, annihilated, wasted, blown into the air! Somehow or other the war has got to stop, Julian. If the politicians won't do it, the people must."

"The people," Julian repeated a little sadly. "Rienzi once trusted in the people."

"There's a difference," Furley protested. "Today the people are all right, but the Rienzi isn't here—My God!"

He broke off suddenly, pursuing another train of thought. He leaned forward.

"Look here," he said, "we'll talk about the fate of that communication later. What about Miss Abbeway?"

"Miss Abbeway," Julian told him, "was in imminent danger last night of arrest as a spy. Against my principles and all my convictions, I have done my best to protect her against the consequences of her ridiculous and inexcusable conduct. I don't know anything about your association, Furley, but I consider you a lot of rotters to allow a girl to take on a job like this."

Furley's eyes flashed in sympathy.

"It was a cowardly action, Julian," he agreed. "I'm hot with shame when I think of it. But don't, for heaven's sake, think I had anything to do with the affair! We have a secret service branch which arranges for those things. It's that skunk Fenn who's responsible. Damn him!"

"Nicholas Fenn, the pacifist!" Julian exclaimed. "So you take vermin like that into your councils!"

"You can't call him too hard a name for me at this moment," Furley muttered.

"Nicholas Fenn," Julian repeated, with a new light in his eyes. "Why, the cable I censored was to him! So he's the arch traitor!"

"Nicholas Fenn is in it," Furley admitted, "although I deny that there's any treason whatever in the affair."

"Don't talk nonsense!" Julian replied. "What about your German hairdresser who was shot this morning?"

"It was a mistake to make use of him," Furley confessed. "Fenn has deceived us all as to the method of our communications. But listen, Julian. You'll be able to get Miss Abbeway out of this?"

"If I don't," Julian replied, "I shall be in it myself, for I've lied myself black in the face already."

"You're a man, for all the starch in you, Julian," Furley declared. "If anything were to happen to that girl, I'd wring Fenn's neck."

"I think she's safe for the present," Julian pronounced. "You see, she isn't in possession of the incriminating document. I took it from her when she was in danger of arrest."

"What are you going to do with it?"

"You can't have much doubt about that," was the composed reply. "I shall go to town to-morrow and hand it over to the proper authorities."

Julian rose to his feet as he spoke. Furley looked at him helplessly.

"How in heaven's name, man," he groaned, "shall I be able to make you see the truth!"

A touch of the winter sunlight was upon Julian's face which, curiously enough, at that moment resembled his father's in its cold, patrician lines. The mention of Nicholas Fenn's name seemed to have transformed him.

"If I were you, Furley," he advised, "for the sake of our friendship, I wouldn't try. There is no consideration in the world which would alter my intentions."

There was the sound of the lifting of the outer latch, a knock at the door. The incoming visitors stood upon no ceremony. Mr. Stenson and Catherine showed themselves upon the threshold.

Mr. Stenson waved aside all ceremony and at once checked Furley's attempt to rise to his feet.

"Pray don't get up, Furley," he begged, shaking hands with him. "I hope you'll forgive such an informal visit. I met Miss Abbeway on my way down to the sea, and when she told me that she was coming to call on you, I asked leave to accompany her."

"You're very welcome, sir," was the cordial response. "It's an honour which I scarcely expected."

Julian found chairs for every one, and Mr. Stenson, recognising intuitively a certain state of tension, continued his good-humoured remarks.

"Miss Abbeway and I," he said, "have been having a most interesting conversation, or rather argument. I find that she is entirely of your way of thinking, Furley. You both belong to the order of what I call puffball politicians."

Catherine laughed heartily at the simile.

"Mr. Stenson is a glaring example," she pointed out, "of those who do not know their own friends. Mr. Furley and I both believe that some time or other our views will appeal to the whole of the intellectual and unselfish world."

"It's a terrible job to get people to think," Furley observed. "They are nearly always busy doing something else."

"And these aristocrats!" Catherine continued, smiling at Julian. "You spoil them so in England, you know. Eton and Oxford are simply terrible in their narrowing effect upon your young men. It's like putting your raw material into a sausage machine."

"Miss Abbeway is very severe this morning," Stenson declared, with unabated good humour. "She has been attacking my policy and my principles during the whole of our walk. Bad luck about your accident, Furley. I suppose we should have met whilst I am down here, if you hadn't developed too adventurous a spirit."

Furley glanced at Julian and smiled.

"I am not so sure about that, sir," he said. "Your host doesn't approve of me very much."

"Do political prejudices exist so far from their home?" Mr. Stenson asked.

"I am afraid my father is rather old-fashioned," Julian confessed.

"You are all old-fashioned—and stiff with prejudice," Furley declared. "Even Orden," he went on, turning to Catherine, "only tolerates me because we ate dinners off the same board when we were both making up our minds to be Lord High Chancellor."

"Our friend Furley," Julian confided, as he leaned across the table and took a cigarette, "has no tact and many prejudices. He does write such rubbish about the aristocracy. I remember an article of his not very long ago, entitled 'Out with our Peers!' It's all very well for a younger son like me to take it lying down, but you could scarcely expect my father to approve. Besides, I believe the fellow's a renegade. I have an idea that he was born in the narrower circles himself."

"That's where you're wrong, then," Furley grunted with satisfaction. "My father was a boot manufacturer in a country village of Leicestershire. I went in for the Bar because he left me pots of money, most of which, by the bye, I seem to have dissipated."

"Chiefly in Utopian schemes for the betterment of his betters," Julian observed drily.

"I certainly had an idea," Furley confessed, "of an asylum for incapable younger sons."

"I call a truce," Julian proposed. "It isn't polite to spar before Miss Abbeway."

"To me," Mr. Stenson declared, "this is a veritable temple of peace. I arrived here literally on all fours. Miss Abbeway has proved to me quite conclusively that as a democratic leader I have missed my vocation."

She looked at him reproachfully. Nevertheless, his words seemed to have brought back to her mind the thrill of their brief but stimulating conversation. A flash of genuine earnestness transformed her face, just as a gleam of wintry sunshine, which had found its way in through the open window, seemed to discover threads of gold in her tightly braided and luxuriant brown hair. Her eyes filled with an almost inspired light:

"Mr. Stenson is scarcely fair to me," she complained. "I did not presume to criticise his statesmanship, only there are some things here which seem pitiful. England should be the ideal democracy of the world. Your laws admit of it, your Government admits of it. Neither birth nor money are indispensable to success. The way is open for the working man to pass even to the Cabinet. And you are nothing of the sort. The cause of the people is not in any country so shamefully and badly represented. You have a bourgeoisie which maintains itself in almost feudal luxury by means of the labour which it employs, and that labour is content to squeak and open its mouth for worms, when it should have the finest fruits of the world. And all this is for want of leadership. Up you come you David Sands, you Phineas Crosses, you Nicholas Fenns, you Thomas Evanses. You each think that you represent Labour, but you don't. You represent trade—the workers at one trade. How they laugh at you, the men who like to keep the government of this country in their own possession! They stretch down a hand to the one who has climbed the highest, they pull him up into the Government, and after that Labour is well quit of him. He has found his place with the gods. Perhaps they will make him a 'Sir' and his wife a 'Lady,' but for him it is all over with the Cause. And so another ten years is wasted, while another man grows up to take his place."

"She's right enough," Furley confessed gloomily. "There is something about the atmosphere of the inner life of politics which has proved fatal to every Labour man who has ever climbed. Paul Fiske wrote the same thing only a few weeks ago. He thought that it was the social atmosphere which we still preserve around our politics. We no sooner catch a clever man, born of the people, than we dress him up like a mummy and put him down at dinner parties and garden parties, to do things he's not accustomed to, and expect him to hold his own amongst people who are not his people. There is something poisonous about it."

"Aren't you all rather assuming," Stenson suggested drily, "that the Labour Party is the only party in politics worth considering?"

"If they knew their own strength," Catherine declared, "they would be the predominant party. Should you like to go to the polls to-day and fight for your seats against them?"

"Heaven forbid!" Mr. Stenson exclaimed. "But then we've made up our mind to one thing—no general election during the war. Afterwards, I shouldn't be at all surprised if Unionists and Liberals and even Radicals didn't amalgamate and make one party."

"To fight Labour," Furley said grimly.

"To keep England great," Mr. Stenson replied. "You must remember that so far as any scheme or program which the Labour Party has yet disclosed, in this country or any other, they are preeminently selfish. England has mighty interests across the seas. A parish-council form of government would very soon bring disaster."

Julian glanced at the clock and rose to his feet.

"I don't want to hurry any one," he said, "but my father is rather a martinet about luncheon."

They all rose. Mr. Stenson turned to Julian.

"Will you go on with Miss Abbeway?" he begged. "I will catch up with you on the marshes. I want to have just a word with Furley."

Julian and his companion crossed the country road and passed through the gate opposite on to the rude track which led down almost to the sea.

"You are very interested in English labour questions, Miss Abbeway," he remarked, "considering that you are only half an Englishwoman."

"It isn't only the English labouring classes in whom I am interested," she replied impatiently. "It is the cause of the people throughout the whole of the world which in my small way I preach."

"Your own country," he continued, a little diffidently, "is scarcely a good advertisement for the cause of social reform."

Her tone trembled with indignation as she answered him.

"My own country," she said, "has suffered for so many centuries from such terrible oppression that the reaction was bound, in its first stages, to produce nothing but chaos. Automatically, all that seems to you unreasonable, wicked even, in a way, horrible—will in the course of time disappear. Russia will find herself. In twenty years' time her democracy will have solved the great problem, and Russia be the foremost republic of the world."

"Meanwhile," he remarked, "she is letting us down pretty badly."

"But you are selfish, you English!" she exclaimed. "You see one of the greatest nations in the world going through its hour of agony, and you think nothing but how you yourselves will be affected! Every thinking person in Russia regrets that this thing should have come to pass at such a time. Yet it is best for you English to look the truth in the face. It wasn't the Russian people who were pledged to you, with whom you were bound in alliance. It was that accursed trick all European politicians have of making secret treaties and secret understandings, building up buffer States, trying to whittle away a piece of the map for yourselves, trying all the time to be dishonest under the shadow of what is called diplomacy. That is what brought the war about. It was never the will of the people. It was the Hohenzollerns and the Romanoffs, the firebrands of the French Cabinet, and your own clumsy, thick-headed efforts to get the best of everybody and yet keep your Nonconformist conscience. The people did not make this war, but it is the people who are going to end it."

They walked in silence for some minutes, he apparently pondering over her last words, she with the cloud passing from her face as, with her head a little thrown back and her eyes half-closed, she sniffed the strong, salty air with an almost voluptuous expression of content. She was perfectly dressed for the country, from her square-toed shoes, which still seemed to maintain some distinction of shape, the perfectly tailored coat and skirt, to the smart little felt hat with its single quill. She walked with the free grace of an athlete, unembarrassed with the difficulties of the way or the gusts which swept across the marshy places, yet not even the strengthening breeze, which as they reached the sea line became almost a gale, seemed to have power to bring even the faintest flush of colour to her cheeks. They reached the long headland and stood looking out at the sea before she spoke again.

"You were very kind to me last night, Mr. Orden," she said, a little abruptly.

"I paid a debt," he reminded her.

"I suppose there is something in that," she admitted. "I really believe that that exceedingly unpleasant person with whom I was brought into temporary association would have killed you if I had allowed it."

"I am inclined to agree with you," he assented. "I saw him very hazily, but a more criminal type of countenance I never beheld."

"So that we are quits," she ventured.

"With a little debt on my side still to be paid."

"Well, there is no telling what demands I may make upon our acquaintance."

"Acquaintance?" he protested.

"Would you like to call it friendship?"

"A very short time ago," he said deliberately, "even friendship would not have satisfied me."

"And now?"

"I dislike mysteries."

"Poor me!" she sighed. "However, you can rid yourself of the shadow of one as soon as you like after luncheon. It would be quite safe now, I think, for me to take back that packet."

"Yes," he assented slowly, "I suppose that it would."

She looked up into his face. Something that she saw there brought her own delicate eyebrows together in a slight frown.

"You will give it me after lunch?" she proposed.

"I think not," was the quiet reply.

"You were only entrusted with it for a time," she reminded him, with ominous calm. "It belongs to me."

"A document received in this surreptitious fashion," he pronounced, "is presumably a treasonable document. I have no intention of returning it to you."

She walked by his side for a few moments in silence. Glancing down into her face, Julian was almost startled. There were none of the ordinary signs of anger there, but an intense white passion, the control of which was obviously costing her a prodigious effort. She touched his fingers with her ungloved hand as she stepped over a stile, and he found them icy cold. All the joy of that unexpectedly sunny morning seemed to have passed.

"I am sorry, Miss Abbeway," he said almost humbly, "that you take my decision so hardly. I ask you to remember that I am just an ordinary, typical Englishman, and that I have already lied for your sake. Will you put yourself in my place?"

They had climbed the little ridge of grass-grown sand and stood looking out seaward. Suddenly all the anger seemed to pass from her face. She lifted her head, her soft brown eyes flashed into his, the little curl of her lips seemed to transform her whole expression. She was no longer the gravely minded prophetess of a great cause, the scheming woman, furious at the prospect of failure. She was suddenly wholly feminine, seductive, a coquette.

"If you were just an ordinary, stupid, stolid Englishman," she whispered, "why did you risk your honour and your safety for my sake? Will you tell me that, dear man of steel?"

Julian leaned even closer over her. She was smiling now frankly into his face, refusing the warning of his burning eyes. Then suddenly, silently, he held her to him and kissed her, unresisting, upon the lips. She made no protest. He even fancied afterwards, when he tried to rebuild in his mind that queer, passionate interlude, that her lips had returned what his had given. It was he who released her—not she who struggled. Yet he understood. He knew that this was a tragedy.

Stenson's voice reached them from the other side of the ridge.

"Come and show me the way across this wretched bit of marsh, Orden. I don't like these deceptive green grasses."

"'Pitfalls for the Politician' or 'Look before you leap'." Julian muttered aimlessly. "Quite right to avoid that spot, sir. Just follow where I am pointing."

Stenson made his laborious way to their side.

"This may be a short cut back to the Hall," he exclaimed, "but except for the view of the sea and this gorgeous air, I think I should have preferred the main road! Help me up, Orden. Isn't it somewhere near here that that little affair happened the other night?"

"This very spot," Julian assented. "Miss Abbeway and I were just speaking of it."

They both glanced towards her. She was standing with her back to them, looking out seawards. She did not move even at the mention of her name.

"A dreary spot at night, I dare say," the Prime Minister remarked, without overmuch interest. "How do we get home from here, Orden? I haven't forgotten your warning about luncheon, and this air is giving me a most lively appetite."

"Straight along the top of this ridge for about three quarters of a mile, sir, to the entrance of the harbour there."

"And then?"

"I have a petrol launch," Julian explained, "and I shall land you practically in the dining room in another ten minutes."

"Let us proceed," Mr. Stenson suggested briskly. "What a queer fellow Miles Furley is! Quite a friend of yours, isn't he, Miss Abbeway?"

"I have seen a good deal of him lately," she answered, walking on and making room for Stenson to fall into step by her side, but still keeping her face a little averted. "A man of many but confused ideas; a man, I should think, who stands an evil chance of muddling his career away."

"We offered him a post in the Government," Stenson ruminated.

"He had just sense enough to refuse that, I suppose," she observed, moving slowly to the right and thereby preventing Julian from taking a place by her side. "Yet," she went on, "I find in him the fault of so many Englishmen, the fault that prevents their becoming great statesmen, great soldiers, or even," she added coolly, "successful lovers."

"And what is that?" Julian demanded.

She remained silent. It was as though she had heard nothing. She caught Mr. Stenson's arm and pointed to a huge white seagull, drifting down the wind above their heads.

"To think," she said, "with that model, we intellectuals have waited nearly two thousand years for the aeroplane!"

VIII

According to plans made earlier in the day, a small shooting party left the Hall immediately after luncheon and did not return until late in the afternoon. Julian, therefore, saw nothing more of Catherine until she came into the drawing-room, a few minutes before the announcement of dinner, wearing a wonderful toilette of pale blue silk, with magnificent pearls around her neck and threaded in her Russian headdress. As is the way with all women of genius, Catherine's complete change of toilette indicated a parallel change in her demeanour. Her interesting but somewhat subdued manner of the previous evening seemed to have vanished. At the dinner table she dominated the conversation. She displayed an intimate acquaintance with every capital of Europe and with countless personages of importance. She exchanged personal reminiscences with Lord Shervinton, who had once been attached to the Embassy at Rome, and with Mr. Hannaway Wells, who had been first secretary at Vienna. She spoke amusingly of Munich, at which place, it appeared, she had first studied art, but dilated, with all the artist's fervour, on her travellings in Spain, on the soft yet wonderfully vivid colouring of the southern cities. She seemed to have escaped altogether from the gravity of which she had displayed traces on the previous evening. She was no longer the serious young woman with a purpose. From the chrysalis she had changed into the butterfly, the brilliant and cosmopolitan young queen of fashion, ruling easily, not with the arrogance of rank, but with the actual gifts of charm and wit. Julian himself derived little benefit from being her neighbour, for the conversation that evening, from first to last, was general. Even after she had left the room, the atmosphere which she had created seemed to linger behind her.

"I have never rightly understood Miss Abbeway," the Bishop declared. "She is a most extraordinarily brilliant young woman."

Lord Shervinton assented.

"To-night you have Catherine Abbeway," he expounded, "as she might have been but for these queer, alternating crazes of hers—art and socialism. Her brain was developed a little too early, and she was unfortunately, almost in her girlhood, thrown in with a little clique of brilliant young Russians who attained a great influence over her. Most of them are in Siberia or have disappeared by now. One Anna

Katinski—was brought back from Tobolsk like a royal princess on the first day of the revolution."

"It is strange," the Earl pronounced didactically, "that a young lady of Miss Abbeway's birth and gifts should espouse the cause of this Labour rabble, a party already cursed with too many leaders."

"A woman, when she takes up a cause," Mr. Hannaway Wells observed, "always seeks either for the picturesque or for something which appeals to the emotions. So long as she doesn't mix with them, the cause of the people has a great deal to recommend it. One can use beautiful phrases, can idealise with a certain amount of logic, and can actually achieve things."

Julian shrugged his shoulders.

"I think we are all a little blind," he remarked, "to the danger in which we stand through the great prosperity of Labour to-day."

The Bishop leaned across the table.

"You have been reading Fiske this week."

"Did I quote?" Julian asked carelessly. "I have a wretched memory. I should never dare to become a politician. I should always be passing off other people's phrases as my own."

"Fiske is quite right in his main contention," Mr. Stenson interposed. "The war is rapidly creating a new class of bourgeoisie. The very differences in the earning of skilled labourers will bring trouble before long—the miner with his fifty or sixty shillings, and the munition worker with his seven or eight pounds—men drawn from the same class."

"England," declared the Earl, indulging in his favourite speech, "was never so contented as when wages were at their lowest."

"Those days will never come again," Mr. Hannaway Wells foretold grimly. "The working man has tasted blood. He has begun to understand his power. Our Ministers have been asleep for a generation. The first of these modern trades unions should have been treated like a secret society in Italy. Look at them now, and what they represent! Fancy what it will mean when they have all learnt to combine!—when Labour produces real leaders!"

"Can any one explain the German democracy?" Lord Shervinton enquired.

"The ubiquitous Fiske was trying to last week in one of the Reviews," Mr. Stenson replied. "His argument was that Germany alone, of all the nations in the world, possessed an extra quality or an extra sense—I forget which he called it—the sense of discipline. It's born in their blood. Generations of military service are responsible for it. Discipline and combination—that might be their motto. Individual thought has been drilled into grooves, just as all individual effort is specialised. The Germans obey because it is their nature to obey. The only question is whether they will stand this, the roughest test they have ever had—whether they'll see the thing through."

"Personally, I think they will," Hannaway Wells pronounced, "but if I should be wrong—if they shouldn't—the French Revolution would be a picnic compared with the German one. It takes a great deal to drive a national idea out of the German mind, but if ever they should understand precisely and exactly how they have been duped for the glorification of their masters—well, I should pity the junkers."

"Do your essays in journalism," the Bishop asked politely, "ever lead you to touch upon Labour subjects, Julian?"

"Once or twice, in a very mild way," was the somewhat diffident reply.

"I had an interesting talk with Furley this morning," the Prime Minister observed. "He tells me that they are thinking of making an appeal to this man Paul Fiske to declare himself. They want a leader—they want one very badly—and thank heavens they don't know where to look for him!"

"But surely," Julian protested, "they don't expect necessarily to find a leader of men in an anonymous contributor to the Reviews? Fiske, when they have found him, may be a septuagenarian, or a man of academic turn of mind, who never leaves his study. 'Paul Fiske' may even be the pseudonym of a woman."

The Earl rose from his place.

"This afternoon," he announced, "I read the latest article of this Paul Fiske. In my opinion he is an exceedingly mischievous person, without the slightest comprehension of the forces which really count in government."

The Bishop's eyes twinkled as he left the room with his hand on his godson's arm.

"It would be interesting," he whispered, "to hear this man Fiske's opinion of your father's last speech in the House of Lords upon land interests!"

It was not until the close of a particularly unsatisfactory evening of uninspiring bridge that Julian saw anything more of Catherine. She came in from the picture gallery, breathless, followed by four or five of the young soldiers, to whom she had been showing the steps of a new dance, and, turning to Julian with an impulsiveness which surprised him, laid her fingers imperatively upon his arm.

"Take me somewhere, please, where we can sit down and talk," she begged, "and give me something to drink."

He led the way into the billiard room and rang the bell.

"You have been overtiring yourself," he said, looking down at her curiously.

"Have I?" she answered. "I don't think so. I used to dance all through the night in Paris and Rome, a few years ago. These young men are so clumsy, though—and I think that I am nervous."

She lay back in her chair and half closed her eyes. A servant brought in the Evian water for which she had asked and a whisky and soda for Julian. She drank thirstily and seemed in a few moments to have overcome her fatigue. She turned to her companion with an air of determination.

"I must speak to you about that packet, Mr. Orden," she insisted.

"Again?"

"I cannot help it. You forget that with me it is a matter of life or death. You must realise that you were only entrusted with it. You are a man of honour. Give it to me."

"I cannot."

"What are you thinking of doing with it, then?"

"I shall take it to London with me to-morrow," he replied, "and hand it over to a friend of mine at the Foreign Office."

"Would nothing that I could do or say," she asked passionately, "influence your decision?"

"Everything that you do or say interests and affects me," he answered simply, "but so far as regards this matter, my duty is clear. You have nothing to fear from my account of how it came into my possession. It would be impossible for me to denounce you for what I fear you are. On the other hand, I cannot allow you the fruits of your enterprise."

"You consider me, I suppose," she observed after a moment's pause, "an enemy spy?"

"You have proved it," he reminded her.

"Of Overman—my confederate," she admitted, "that was true. Of me it is not. I am an honest intermediary between the honest people of Germany and England."

"There can be no communication between the two countries during wartime, except through official channels," he declared.

Her eyes flashed. She seemed in the throes of one of those little bursts of tempestuous passion which sometimes assailed her.

"You talk—well, as you might be supposed to talk!" she exclaimed, breaking off with an effort. "What have official channels done to end this war? I am not here to help either side. I represent simply humanity. If you destroy or hand over to the Government that packet, you will do your country an evil turn."

He shook his head.

"I am relieved to hear all that you say," he told her, "and I am heartily glad to think that you do not look upon yourself as Overman's associate. On the other hand, you must know that any movement towards peace, except through the authorised channels, is treason to the country."

"If only you were not the Honourable Julian Orden, the son of an English peer!" she groaned. "If only you had not been to Eton and to Oxford! If only you were a man, a man of the people, who could understand!"

"Neither my birth nor my education," he assured her, "have affected my present outlook upon life."

"Pooh!" she scoffed. "You talk like a stiffened sheet of foolscap! I am to leave here to-morrow, then, without my packet?"

"You must certainly leave—when you do leave—without that," he assented. "There is one thing, however, which I very sincerely hope that you will leave behind you."

"And that?"

"Your forgiveness."

"My forgiveness for what?" she asked, after a moment's pause.

"For my rashness this morning."

Her eyes grew a little larger.

"Because you kissed me?" she observed, without flinching. "I have nothing to forgive. In fact," she went on, "I think that I should have had more to forgive if you had not."

He was puzzled and yet encouraged. She was always bewildering him by her sudden changes from the woman of sober thoughtfulness to the woman of feeling, the woman eager to give, eager to receive. At that moment it seemed as though her sex possessed her to the exclusion of everything outside. Her eyes were soft and filled with the desire of love, her lips sweet and tremulous. She had suddenly created a new atmosphere around her, an atmosphere of bewildering and passionate femininity.

"Won't you tell me, please, what you mean?" he begged.

"Isn't it clear?" she answered, very softly but with a suspicion of scorn in her low tones. "You kissed me because I deliberately invited it. I know that quite well. My anger—and I have been angry about it—is with myself."

He was a little taken aback. Her perfect naturalness was disarming, a little confusing.

"You certainly did seem provocative," he confessed, "but I ought to have remembered."

"You are very stupid," she sighed. "I deliberately invited your embrace. Your withholding it would simply have added to my humiliation. I am furious with myself, simply because, although I have lived a great part of my life with men, on equal terms with them, working with them, playing with them, seeing more of them at all times than of my own sex, such a thing has never happened to me before."

"I felt that," he said simply.

For a moment her face shone. There was a look of gratitude in her eyes. Her impulsive grasp of his hand left his fingers tingling.

"I am glad that you understood," she murmured. "Perhaps that will help me just a little. For the rest, if you wish to be very kind, you will forget."

"If I cannot do that," he promised, "I will at least turn the key upon my memories."

"Do more than that," she begged. "Throw the key into the sea, or whatever oblivion you choose to conjure up. Moments such as those have no place in my life. There is one purpose there more intense than anything else, that very purpose which by some grim irony of fate it seems to be within your power to destroy."

He remained silent. Ordinary expressions of regret seemed too inadequate. Besides, the charm of the moment was passing. The other side of her was reasserting itself.

"I suppose," she went on, a little drearily, "that even if I told you upon my honour, of my certain knowledge, that the due delivery of that packet might save the lives of thousands of your countrymen, might save hearts from breaking, homes from becoming destitute—even if I told you all this, would it help me in my prayer?"

"Nothing could help you," he assured her, "but your whole confidence, and even then I fear that the result would be the same."

"Oh, but you are very hard!" she murmured. "My confidence belongs to others. It is not mine alone to give you."

"You see," he explained, "I know beforehand that you are speaking the truth as you see it. I know beforehand that any scheme in which you are engaged is for the benefit of our fellow creatures and not for their harm. But alas! you make yourself the judge of these things, and there are times when individual effort is the most dangerous thing in life."

"If you were any one else!" she sighed.

"Why be prejudiced about me?" he protested. "Believe me, I am not a frivolous person. I, too, think of life and its problems. You yourself are an aristocrat. Why should not I as well as you have sympathy and feeling for those who suffer?"

"I am a Russian," she reminded him, "and in Russia it is different. Besides, I am no longer an aristocrat. I am a citizeness of the world. I have eschewed everything in life except one thing, and for that I have worked with all my heart and strength. As for you, what have you done? What is your record?"

"Insignificant, I fear," he admitted. "You see, a very promising start at the Bar was somewhat interfered with by my brief period of soldiering."

"At the present moment you have no definite career," she declared. "You have even been wasting your time censoring."

"I am returning now to my profession."

"Your profession!" she scoffed. "That means you will spend your time wrangling with a number of other bewigged and narrow-minded people about uninteresting legal technicalities which lead nowhere and which no one cares about."

"There is my journalism."

"You have damned it with your own phrase 'hack journalism'!"

"I may enter Parliament."

"Yes, to preserve your rights," she retorted.

"I am afraid," he sighed, "that you haven't a very high opinion of me."

"It is within your power to make me look upon you as the bravest, the kindest, the most farseeing of men," she declared.

He shook his head.

"I decline to think that you would think any the better of me for committing a dishonourable action for your sake."

"Try me," she begged, her hand resting once more upon his. "If you want my kind feelings, my everlasting gratitude, they are yours. Give me that packet."

"That is impossible," he declared uncompromisingly. "If you wish to alter my attitude with regard to it, you must tell me exactly from whom it comes, what it contains, and to whom it goes."

"You ask more than is possible.. You make me almost sorry—"

"Sorry for what?"

"Sorry that I saved your life," she said boldly. "Why should I not be? There are many who will suffer, many who will lose their lives because of your obstinacy."

"If you believe that, confide in me."

She shook her head sadly.

"If only you were different!"

"I am a human being," he protested. "I have sympathies and heart. I would give my life willingly to save any carnage."

"I could never make you understand," she murmured hopelessly. "I shall not try. I dare not risk failure. Is this room hot, or is it my fancy? Could we have a window open?"

"By all means."

He crossed the room and lifted the blind from before one of the high windows which opened seawards. In the panel of the wall, between the window to which he addressed himself and the next one, was a tall, gilt mirror, relic of the days, some hundreds of years ago, when the apartment had been used as a drawing-room. Julian, by the merest accident, for the pleasure of a stolen glance at Catherine, happened to look in it as he leaned over towards the window fastening. For a single moment he stood rigid. Catherine had risen to her feet and, without the slightest evidence of any fatigue, was leaning, tense and alert, over the tray on which his untouched whisky and soda was placed. Her hand was outstretched. He saw a little stream of white powder fall into the tumbler. An intense and sickening feeling of disappointment almost brought a groan to his lips. He conquered himself with an effort, however, opened the window a few inches, and returned to his place. Catherine was lying back, her eyes half-closed, her arms hanging listlessly on either side of her chair.

"Is that better?" he enquired.

"Very much," she assured him. "Still, I think that if you do not mind, I will go to bed. I am troubled with a very rare attack of nerves. Drink your whisky and soda, and then will you take me into the drawing-room?"

He played with his tumbler thoughtfully. His first impulse was to drop it. Intervention, however, was at hand. The door opened, and the Princess entered with Lord Shervinton.

"At last!" the former exclaimed. "I have been looking for you everywhere, child. I am sure that you are quite tired out, and I insist upon your going to bed."

"Finish your whisky and soda," Catherine begged Julian, "and I will lean on your arm as far as the staircase."

Fate stretched out her right hand to help him. The Princess took possession of her niece.

"I shall look after you myself," she insisted. "Mr. Orden is wanted to play billiards. Lord Shervinton is anxious for a game."

"I shall be delighted," Julian answered promptly.

He moved to the door and held it open. Catherine gave him her fingers and a little half-doubtful smile.

"If only you were not so cruelly obstinate!" she sighed.

He found no words with which to answer her. The shock of his discovery was still upon him.

"You'll give me thirty in a hundred, Julian," Lord Shervinton called out cheerfully. "And shut that door as soon as you can, there's a good fellow. There's a most confounded draught."

IX

It was at some nameless hour in the early morning when Julian's vigil came to an end, when the handle of his door was slowly turned, and the door itself pushed open and closed again. Julian, lying stretched upon his bed, only half prepared for the night, with a dressing gown wrapped around him, continued to breathe heavily, his eyes half-closed, listening intently to the fluttering of light garments, the soft, almost noiseless footfall of light feet. He heard her shake out his dinner coat, try the pockets, heard the stealthy opening and closing of the drawers in his wardrobe. Presently the footsteps drew near to his bed. For a moment he was obliged to set his teeth. A little waft of peculiar, unanalysable perfume, half-fascinating, half-repellent, came to him with a sense of disturbing familiarity. She paused by his bedside. He felt her hand steal under the pillow, which his head scarcely touched; search the pockets of his dressing gown, search even the bed. He listened to her soft breathing. The consciousness of her close and intimate presence affected him in an inexplicable manner. Presently, to his intense relief, she glided away from his immediate neighbourhood, and the moment for which he had waited came. He heard her retreating footsteps pass through the communicating door into his little sitting room, where he had purposely left a light burning. He slipped softly from the bed and followed her. She was bending over an open desk as he crossed the threshold. He closed the door and stood with his back to it.

"Much warmer," he said, "only, you see, it isn't there."

She started violently at the sound of his voice, but she did not immediately turn around. When she did so, her demeanour was almost a shock to him. There was no sign of nervousness or apology in her manner. Her eyes flashed at him angrily. She wore a loose red wrap trimmed with white fur, a dishabille unusually and provokingly attractive.

"So you were shamming sleep!" she exclaimed indignantly.

"Entirely," he admitted.

Neither spoke for a moment. Her eyes fell upon a tumbler of whisky and soda, which stood on a round table drawn up by the side of his easy-chair.

"I have not come to bed thirsty," he assured her. "I had another one downstairs—to which I helped myself. This one I brought up to try if

I could remember sufficient of my chemistry to determine its contents. I have been able to decide, to my great relief, that your intention was probably to content yourself with plunging me into only temporary slumber."

"I wanted you out of the way whilst I searched your rooms," she told him coolly. "If you were not such an obstinate, pig-headed, unkind, prejudiced person, it would not have been necessary."

"Dear me!" he murmured. "Am I all that? Won't you sit down?"

For a moment she looked as though she were about to strike him with the electric torch which she was carrying. With a great effort of self-control, however, she changed her mind and threw herself into his easy-chair with a little gesture of recklessness. Julian seated himself opposite to her. Although she kept her face as far as possible averted, he realised more than ever in those few moments that she was really an extraordinarily beautiful person. Her very attitude was full of an angry grace. The quivering of her lips was the only sign of weakness. Her eyes were filled with cold resentment.

"Well," she said, "I am your prisoner. I listen."

"You are after that packet, I suppose?"

"What sagacity!" she scoffed. "I trusted you with it, and you behaved like a brute. You kept it. It has nothing to do with you. You have no right to it."

"Let us understand one another, once and for all," he suggested. "I will not even discuss the question of rightful or wrongful possession. I have the packet, and I am going to keep it. You cannot cajole it out of me, you cannot steal it from me. To-morrow I shall take it to London and deliver it to my friend at the Foreign Office. Nothing could induce me to change my mind."

She seemed suddenly to be caught up in the vortex of a new emotion. All the bitterness passed from her expression. She fell on her knees by his side, sought his hands, and lifted her face, full of passionate entreaty, to his. Her eyes were dimmed with tears, her voice piteous.

"Do not be so cruel, so hard," she begged. "I swear before Heaven that there is no treason in those papers, that they are the one necessary link in a great, humanitarian scheme. Be generous, Mr. Orden. Julian! Give it back to me. It is mine. I swear—"

His hands gripped her shoulders. She was conscious that he was looking past her, and that there was horror in his eyes. The words died away on her lips. She, too, turned her head. The door of the sitting room had been opened from outside. Lord Maltenby was standing there in his dressing gown, his hand stretched out behind him as though to keep some one from following him.

"Julian," he demanded sternly, "what is the meaning of this?"

For a moment Julian was speechless, bereft of words, or sense of movement. Catherine still knelt there, trembling. Then Lord Maltenby was pushed unceremoniously to one side. It was the Princess who entered.

"Catherine!" she screamed. "Catherine!"

The girl rose slowly to her feet. The Princess was leaning on the back of a chair, dabbing her eyes with a handkerchief and sobbing hysterically. Lord Shervinton's voice was heard outside.

"What the devil is all this commotion?" he demanded.

He, too, crossed the threshold and remained transfixed. The Earl closed the door firmly and stood with his back against it.

"Come," he said, "we will have no more spectators to this disgraceful scene. Julian, kindly remember you are not in your bachelor apartments. You are in the house over which your mother presides. Have you any reason to offer, or excuse to urge, why I should not ask this young woman to leave at daybreak?"

"I have no excuse, sir," Julian answered, "I certainly have a reason."

"Name it?"

"Because you would be putting an affront upon the lady who has promised to become my wife. I am quite aware that her presence in my sitting room is unusual, but under the circumstances I do not feel called upon to offer a general explanation. I shall say nothing beyond the fact that a single censorious remark will be considered by me as an insult to my affianced wife."

The Princess abandoned her chorus of mournful sounds and dried her eyes. Lord Waltenby was speechless.

"But why all this mystery?" the Princess asked pitifully. "It is a great event, this. Why did you not tell me, Catherine, when you came to my room?"

"There has been some little misunderstanding," Julian explained. "It is now removed. It brought us," he added, "very near tragedy. After what I have told you, I beg whatever may seem unusual to you in this visit with which Catherine has honoured me will be forgotten."

Lord Maltenby drew a little breath of relief. Fortunately, he missed that slight note of theatricality in Julian's demeanour which might have left the situation still dubious.

"Very well, then, Julian," he decided, "there is nothing more to be said upon the matter. Miss Abbeway, you will allow me to escort you to your room. Such further explanations as you may choose to offer us can be very well left now until the morning."

"You will find that the whole blame for this unconventional happening devolves upon me," Julian declared.

"It was entirely my fault," Catherine murmured repentantly. "I am so sorry to have given any one cause for distress. I do not know, even now—"

She turned towards Julian. He leaned forward and raised her fingers to his lips.

"Catherine," he said, "every one is a little overwrought. Our misunderstanding is finished. Princess, I shall try to win your forgiveness to-morrow."

The Princess smiled faintly.

"Catherine is so unusual," she complained.

Julian held open the door, and they all filed away down the corridor, from which Lord Shervinton had long since beat a hurried retreat. He stood there until they reached the bend. Catherine, who was leaning on his father's arm, turned around. She waved her hand a little irresolutely. She was too far off for him to catch her expression, but there was something pathetic in her slow, listless walk, from which all the eager grace of a few hours ago seemed to have departed.

It was not until they were nearing London, on the following afternoon, that Catherine awoke from a lethargy during which she had spent the greater portion of the journey. From her place in the corner seat of the compartment in which they had been undisturbed since leaving Wells, she studied her companion through half-closed eyes. Julian was reading an article in one of the Reviews and remained entirely unconscious of her scrutiny. His forehead was puckered, his mouth a little contemptuous. It was obvious that he did not wholly approve of what he was reading.

Catherine, during those few hours of solitude, was conscious of a subtle, slowly growing change in her mental attitude towards her companion. Until the advent of those dramatic hours at Maltenby, she had regarded him as a pleasant, even a charming acquaintance, but as belonging to a type with which she was entirely and fundamentally out of sympathy. The cold chivalry of his behaviour on the preceding night and the result of her own reflections as she sat there studying him made her inclined to doubt the complete accuracy of her first judgment. She found something unexpectedly intellectual and forceful in his present concentration,—in the high, pale forehead, the deep-set but alert eyes. His long, loose frame was yet far from ungainly; his grey tweed suit and well-worn brown shoes the careless attire of a man who has no need to rely on his tailor for distinction. His hands, too, were strong and capable. She found herself suddenly wishing that the man himself were different, that he belonged to some other and more congenial type.

Julian, in course of time, laid down the Review which he had been studying and looked out of the window.

"We shall be in London in three quarters of an hour," he announced politely.

She sat up and yawned, produced her vanity case, peered into the mirror, and used her powder puff with the somewhat piquant assurance of the foreigner. Then she closed her dressing case with a snap, pulled down her veil, and looked across at him.

"And how," she asked demurely, "does my fiance propose to entertain me this evening?"

He raised his eyebrows.

"With the exception of one half-hour," he replied unexpectedly, "I am wholly at your service."

"I am exacting," she declared. "I demand that half-hour also."

"I am afraid that I could not allow anything to interfere with one brief call which I must pay."

"In Downing Street?"

"Precisely!"

"You go to visit your friend at the Foreign Office?"

"Immediately I have called at my rooms."

She looked away from him out of the window. Beneath her veil her eyes were a little misty. She saw nothing of the trimly partitioned fields, the rolling pastoral country. Before her vision tragedies seemed to pass,—the blood-stained paraphernalia of the battlefield, the empty, stricken homes, the sobbing women in black, striving to comfort their children whilst their own hearts were breaking. When she turned away from the window, her face was hardened. Once more she found herself almost hating the man who was her companion. Whatever might come afterwards, at that moment she had the sensations of a murderess.

"You may know when you sleep to-night," she exclaimed, "that you will be the blood-guiltiest man in the world!"

"I would not dispute the title," he observed politely, "with your friend the Hohenzollern."

"He is not my friend," she retorted, her tone vibrating with passion. "I am a traitress in your eyes because I have received a communication from Germany. From whom does it come, do you think? From the Court? From the Chancellor or one of his myrmidons? Fool! It comes from those who hate the whole military party. It comes from the Germany whose people have been befooled and strangled throughout the war. It comes from the people whom your politicians have sought to reach and failed."

"The suggestion is interesting," he remarked coldly, "but improbable."

"Do you know," she said, leaning a little forward and looking at him fixedly, "if I were really your fiancee—worse! if I were really your wife—I think that before long I should be a murderess!"

"Do you dislike me as much as all that?"

"I hate you! I think you are the most pigheaded, obstinate, self-satisfied, ignorant creature who ever ruined a great cause."

He accepted the lash of her words without any sign of offence,—seemed, indeed, inclined to treat them reflectively.

"Come," he protested, "you have wasted a lot of breath in abusing me. Why not justify it? Tell me the story of yourself and those who are associated with you in this secret correspondence with Germany? If you are working for a good end, let me know of it. You blame me for judging you, for maintaining a certain definite poise. You are not reasonable, you know."

"I blame you for being what you are," she answered breathlessly. "If you were a person who understood, who felt the great stir of humanity outside your own little circle, who could look across your seas and realise that nationality is accidental and that the brotherhood of man throughout the world is the only real fact worthy of consideration—ah! if you could realise these things, I could talk, I could explain."

"You judge me in somewhat arbitrary fashion."

"I judge you from your life, your prejudices, even the views which you have expressed."

"There are some of us," he reminded her, "to whom reticence is a national gift. I like what you said just now. Why should you take it for granted that I am a narrow squireen? Why shouldn't you believe that I, too, may feel the horror of these days?"

"You feel it personally but not impersonally," she cried. "You feel it intellectually but not with your heart. You cannot see that a kindred soul lives in the Russian peasant and the German labourer, the British toiler and the French artificer. They are all pouring out their blood for the sake of their dream, a politician's dream. Freedom isn't won by wars. It must be won, if ever, by moral sacrifice and not with blood."

"Then explain to me," he begged, "exactly what you are doing? What your reason is for being in communication with the German Government? Remember that the dispatch I intercepted came from no private person in Germany. It came from those in authority."

"That again is not true," she replied. "I would ask for permission to explain all these things to you, if it were not so hopeless."

"The case of your friends will probably be more hopeless still," he reminded her, "after to-night."

She shrugged her shoulders.

"We shall see," she said solemnly. "The Russian revolution surprised no one. Perhaps an English revolution would shake even your self-confidence."

He made no reply. Her blood tingled, and she could have struck him for the faint smile, almost of amusement, which for a moment parted his lips. He was already on his feet, collecting their belongings.

"Can you help me," he asked, "with reference to the explanations which it will be necessary to make to your aunt and to my own people? We left this morning, if you remember, in order that you might visit the Russian Embassy and announce our betrothal. You are, I believe, under an engagement to return and stay with my mother."

"I cannot think about those things to-day," she replied. "You may take it that I am tired and that you had business. You know my address. May I be favoured with yours?"

He handed her a card and scribbled a telephone number upon it. They were in the station now, and their baggage in the hands of separate porters. She walked slowly down the platform by his side.

"Will you allow me to say," he ventured, "how sorry I am—for all this?"

The slight uncertainty of his speech pleased her. She looked up at him with infinite regret. As they neared the barrier, she held out her hand.

"I, too, am more sorry than I can tell you;" she said a little tremulously. "Whatever may come, that is how I feel myself. I am sorry."

They separated almost upon the words. Catherine was accosted by a man at whom Julian glanced for a moment in surprise, a man whose dress and bearing, confident though it was, clearly indicated some other status in life. He glanced at Julian with displeasure, a displeasure which seemed to have something of jealousy in its composition. Then he grasped Catherine warmly by the hand.

"Welcome back to London, Miss Abbeway! Your news?"

Her reply was inaudible. Julian quickened his pace and passed out of the station ahead of them.

X

The Bishop and the Prime Minister met, one afternoon a few days later, at the corner of Horse Guards Avenue. The latter was looking brown and well, distinctly the better for his brief holiday. The Bishop, on the contrary, was pale and appeared harassed. They shook hands and exchanged for a moment the usual inanities.

"Tell me, Mr. Stenson," the Bishop asked earnestly, "what is the meaning of all this Press talk, about peace next month? I have heard a hint that it was inspired."

"You are wrong," was the firm reply. "I have sent my private secretary around to a few of the newspapers this morning. It just happens to be the sensation, of the moment, and it's fed all the time from the other side."

"There is nothing in it, then, really?"

"Nothing whatever. Believe me, Bishop—and there is no one feeling the strain more than I am—the time has not yet come for peace."

"You politicians!" the Bishop sighed. "Do you sometimes forget, I wonder, that even the pawns you move are human?"

"I can honestly say that I, at any rate, have never forgotten it," Mr. Stenson answered gravely. "There isn't a man in my Government who has a single personal feeling in favour of, or a single benefit to gain, by the continuance of this ghastly war. On the other hand, there is scarcely one who does not realise that the end is not yet. We have pledged our word, the word of the English nation, to a peace based only upon certain contingencies. Those contingencies the enemy is not at present prepared to accept. There is no immediate reason why he should."

"But are you sure of that?" the Bishop ventured doubtfully. "When you speak of Germany, you speak of William of Hohenzollern and his clan. Is that Germany? Is theirs the voice of the people?"

"I would be happy to believe that it was not," Mr. Stenson replied, "but if that is the case, let them give us a sign of it."

"That sign," declared the Bishop, with a gleam of hopefulness in his tone, "may come, and before long."

The two men were on the point of parting. Mr. Stenson turned and walked a yard or two with his companion.

"By the bye, Bishop," he enquired, "have you heard any rumours concerning the sudden disappearance of our young friend Julian Orden?"

The Bishop for a moment was silent. A passer-by glanced at the two men sympathetically. Of the two, he thought, it was the man in spiritual charge of a suffering people who showed more sign of the strain.

"I have heard rumours," the Bishop acknowledged. "Tell me what you know?"

"Singularly little," Mr. Stenson replied. "He left Maltenby with Miss Abbeway the day after their engagement, and, according to the stories which I have heard, arranged to dine with her that night. She came to call for him and found that he had disappeared. According to his servant, he simply walked out in morning clothes, soon after six o'clock, without leaving any message, and never returned. On the top of that, though, there followed, as I expect you have heard, some very insistent police enquiries as to Orden's doings on the night he spent with his friend Miles Furley. There is no doubt that a German submarine was close to Blakeney harbour that night and that a communication of some sort was landed."

"It seems absurd to connect Julian with any idea of treasonable communication with Germany," the Bishop said slowly. "A more typical young Englishman of his class I never met."

"Up to a certain point I agree with you," Mr. Stenson confessed, "but there are some further rumours to which I cannot allude, concerning Julian. Orden, which are, to say the least of it, surprising."

The two men came to a standstill once more.

Stenson laid his hand upon his companion's shoulder. "Come," he went on, "I know what is the matter with you, my friend. Your heart is too big. The cry of the widow and the children lingers too long in your ears. Remember some of your earlier sermons at the beginning of the war. Remember how wonderfully you spoke one morning at St. Paul's upon the spirituality to be developed by suffering, by sacrifice. 'The hand which chastises also purifies.' Wasn't that what you said? You probably didn't know that I was one of your listeners, even—I myself, in those days, scarcely looked upon the war as I do now. I remember crawling in at the side door of the Cathedral and sitting unrecognised on a hard chair. It was a great congregation, and I was far away in the background, but I heard. I remember the rustle, too, the little moaning, indrawn breath of emotion when the people rose to their feet. Take heart, Bishop. I will remind you once more of your own words 'These are the days of purification.'"

The two men separated. The Bishop walked thoughtfully towards the Strand, his hands clasped behind his back, the echo of those quoted words of his still in his ear. As he came to the busy crossing, he raised his head and looked around him.

"Perhaps," he murmured, "my eyes have been closed. Perhaps there are things to be seen."

He called a taxicab and, giving the man some muttered directions, was driven slowly down the Strand, looking eagerly first on one side of the way and then on the other. It was approaching the luncheon hour and the streets were thronged. Here seemed to be the meeting place of the Colonial troops,—long, sinewy men, many of them, with bronzed faces and awkward gait. They elbowed their way along, side by side with the queerest collection of people in the world. They stopped and talked in little knots, they entered and left the public houses, stood about outside the restaurants. Here and there they walked arm in arm with women. Taxicabs were turning in at the Savoy, taxicabs and private cars. Young ladies of the stage, sometimes alone, very often escorted, were everywhere in evidence. The life of London was flowing on in very much the same channels. There were few, if any signs of that thing for which he sought. The taxicab turned westwards, crossed Piccadilly Circus and proceeded along Piccadilly, its solitary occupant still gazing into the faces of the people with that same consuming interest. It was all the same over again—the smiling throngs entering and leaving the restaurants, the smug promenaders, the stream of gaily dressed women and girls. Bond Street was even more crowded with shoppers and loiterers. The shop windows were as full as ever, the toilettes of the women as wonderful. Mankind, though khaki-clad, was plentiful. The narrow thoroughfare was so crowded that his taxicab went only at a snail's crawl, and occasionally he heard scraps of conversation. Two pretty girls were talking to two young men in uniform.

"What a rag last night! I didn't get home till three!"

"Dick never got home at all. Still missing!"

"Evie and I are worn out with shopping. Everything's twice as expensive, but one simply can't do without."

"I shouldn't do without anything, these days. One never knows how long it may last."

The taxicab moved on, and the Bishop's eyes for a moment were half-closed. The voices followed him, however. Two women, leading curled and pampered toy dogs, were talking at the corner of the street.

"Sugar, my dear?" one was saying. "Why, I laid in nearly a hundredweight, and I can always get what I want now. The shopkeepers know that they have to have your custom after the war. It's only the people who can't afford to buy much at a time who are really inconvenienced."

"Of course, it's awfully sad about the war, and all that, but one has to think of oneself. Harry told me last night that after paying all the income tax he couldn't get out of, and excess profits; he is still—"

The voices dropped to a whisper. The Bishop thrust his head out of the window.

"Drive me to Tothill Street, Westminster," he directed. "As quickly as possible, please."

The man turned up a side street and drove off. Still the Bishop watched, only by now the hopefulness had gone from his face. He had sought for something of which there had been no sign.

He dismissed his taxicab in front of a large and newly finished block of buildings in the vicinity of Westminster. A lift man conducted him to the seventh floor, and a commissionaire ushered him into an already crowded waiting room. A youth, however, who had noticed the Bishop's entrance, took him in charge, and, conducting him through two other crowded rooms, knocked reverently at the door of an apartment at the far end of the suite. The door was opened, after a brief delay, by a young man of unpleasant appearance, who gazed suspiciously at the distinguished visitor through heavy spectacles.

"The Bishop wishes to see Mr. Fenn," his guide announced.

"Show him in at once," a voice from the middle of the room directed. "You can go and have your lunch, Johnson."

The Bishop found himself alone with the man whom he had come to visit,—a moderately tall, thin figure, badly-dressed, with a drooping moustache, bright eyes and good forehead, but peevish expression. He stood up while he shook hands with the Bishop and motioned him to a chair.

"First time you've honoured us, Bishop," he remarked, with the air of one straining after an equality which he was far from feeling.

"I felt an unconquerable impulse to talk with you," the Bishop admitted. "Tell me your news?"

"Everything progresses," Nicholas Fenn declared confidently. "The last eleven days have seen a social movement in this country, conducted with absolute secrecy, equivalent in its portentous issues to the greatest revolution of modern times. For the first time in history, Bishop, the united voice of the people has a chance of making itself heard."

"Mr. Fenn," the Bishop said, "you have accomplished a wonderful work. Now comes the moment when we must pause and think. We must be absolutely and entirely certain that the first time that voice is heard it is heard in a righteous cause."

"Is there a more righteous cause in the world than the cause of peace?" Fenn asked sharply.

"Not if that peace be just and reasonable," the Bishop replied, "not if that peace can bring to an end this horrible and bloody struggle."

"We shall see to that," Fenn declared, with a self-satisfied air.

"You have by now, I suppose, the terms proposed by your—your kindred body in Germany?"

Nicholas Fenn stroked his moustache. There was a frown upon his forehead.

"I expect to have them at any moment," he said, "but to tell you the truth, at the present moment they are not available."

"But I thought—"

"Just so," the other interrupted. "The document, however, was not where we expected to find it."

"Surely that is a very serious complication?"

"It will mean a certain delay if we don't succeed in getting hold of it," Fenn admitted. "We intend to be firm about the matter, though."

The Bishop's expression was troubled.

"Julian Orden," he said, "is my godson."

"Necessity knows neither friendship nor relationship," Fenn pronounced didactically. "Better ask no questions, sir. These details do not concern you."

"They concern my conscience," was the grave reply. "Ours is an earnest spiritual effort for peace, a taking away from the hands of the politicians of a great human question which they have proved themselves unable to handle. We should look, therefore, with peculiar care to the means we adopt."

Nicholas Fenn nodded. He lit a very pungent cigarette from a paper packet by his side.

"You and I, Bishop," he said, "are pacifists in the broadest meaning of the word, but that does not mean that we may not sometimes have to use force to attain our object. We have a department which alone is concerned with the dealing of such matters. It is that department which has undertaken the forwarding and receipt of all communications between ourselves and our friends across the North Sea. Its operations are entirely secret, even from the rest of the Council. It will deal with Julian Orden. It is best for you not to interfere, or even to have cognisance of what is going on."

"I cannot agree," the Bishop protested. "An act of unchristian violence would be a flaw in the whole superstructure which we are trying to build up."

"Let us discuss some other subject," Fenn proposed.

"Pardon me," was the firm reply. "I have come here to discuss this one."

Nicholas Fenn looked down at the table. His expression was not altogether pleasant.

"Your position with us, sir," he said, "although much appreciated, does not warrant your interference in executive details."

"Nevertheless," the Bishop insisted, "you must please treat me reasonably in this matter, Mr. Fenn. Remember I am not altogether extinct as a force amongst your followers. I have three mass meetings to address this week, and there is the sermon next Sunday at Westminster Abbey, at which it has been agreed that I shall strike the first note of warning. I am a helper, I believe, worth considering, and there is no man amongst you who risks what I risk."

"Exactly what are you asking from me?" Fenn demanded, after a moment's deliberation.

"I wish to know the whereabouts and condition of Julian Orden."

"The matter is one which is being dealt with by our secret service department," Fenn replied, "but I see no reason why I should not give you all reasonable information. The young man in question asked for trouble, and to a certain extent he has found it."

"I understand," the Bishop reminded his companion, "that he has very nearly, if not altogether, compromised himself in his efforts to shield Miss Abbeway."

"That may be so," Fenn admitted, "but it doesn't alter the fact that he refuses to return to her the packet which she entrusted to his care."

"And he is still obdurate?"

"Up to now, absolutely so. Perhaps," Fenn added, with a slightly malicious smile, "you would like to try what you can do with him yourself?"

The Bishop hesitated.

"Julian Orden," he said, "is a young man of peculiarly stubborn type, but if I thought that my exhortations would be of any benefit, I would not shrink from trying them, whatever it might cost me."

"Better have a try, then," Fenn suggested. "If we do not succeed within the next twenty-four hours, I shall give you an order to see him. I don't mind confessing," he went on confidentially, "that the need for the production of that document is urgent, apart from the risk we run of having our plans forestalled if it should fall into the hands of the Government."

"I presume that Miss Abbeway has already done her best?"

"She has worn herself out with persuasions."

"Has he himself been told the truth?"

Fenn shook his head.

"From your own knowledge of the young man, do you think that it would be of any use? Even Miss Abbeway is forced to admit that any one less likely to sympathise with our aims it would be impossible to find. At the same time, if we do arrange an interview for you, use any arguments you can think of. To tell you the truth, our whole calculations have been upset by not discovering the packet upon his person. He was on his way to Downing Street when our agents intervened, and we never doubted that he would have it with him. When will it be convenient for you to pay your visit?"

"At any time you send for me," the Bishop replied. "Meanwhile, Mr. Fenn, before I leave I want to remind you once more of the original purpose of my call upon you."

Fenn frowned a little peevishly as he rose to usher his visitor out.

"Miss Abbeway has already extorted a foolish promise from us," he said. "The young man's safety for the present is not in question."

The Bishop, more from custom than from any appetite, walked across the Park to the Athenaeum. Mr. Hannaway Wells accosted him in the hall.

"This is a world of rumours," he remarked with a smile. "I have just heard that Julian Orden, of all men in the world, has been shot as a German spy."

The Bishop smiled with dignity.

"You may take it from me," he said gravely, "that the rumour is untrue."

XI

Nicholas Fenn, although civilisation had laid a heavy hand upon him during the last few years, was certainly not a man whose outward appearance denoted any advance in either culture or taste. His morning clothes, although he had recently abandoned the habit of dealing at a ready-made emporium, were neither well chosen nor well worn. His evening attire was, if possible, worse. He met Catherine that evening in the lobby of what he believed to be a fashionable grillroom, in a swallow-tailed coat, a badly fitting shirt with a single stud-hole, a black tie, a collar which encircled his neck like a clerical band, and ordinary walking boots. She repressed a little shiver as she shook hands and tried to remember that this was not only the man whom several millions of toilers had chosen to be their representative, but also the duly appointed secretary of the most momentous assemblage of human beings in the world's history.

"I hope I am not late," she said. "I really do not care much about dining out, these days, but your message was so insistent."

"One must have relaxation," he declared. "The weight of affairs all day long is a terrible strain. Shall we go in?"

They entered the room and stood looking aimlessly about them, Fenn having, naturally enough, failed to realise the necessity of securing a table. A maitre d'hotel, however, recognised Catherine and hastened to their rescue. She conversed with the man for a few minutes in French, while her companion listened admiringly, and finally, at his solicitation, herself ordered the dinner.

"The news, please, Mr. Fenn?" she asked, as soon as the man had withdrawn.

"News?" he repeated. "Oh, let's leave it alone for a time! One gets sick of shop."

She raised her eyebrows a little discouragingly. She was dressed with extraordinary simplicity, but the difference in caste between the two supplied a problem for many curious observers.

"Why should we talk of trifles," she demanded, "when we both have such a great interest in the most wonderful subject in the world?"

"What is the most wonderful subject in the world?" he asked impressively.

"Our cause, of course," she answered firmly, "the cause of all the peoples—Peace."

"One labours the whole day long for that," he grumbled. "When the hour for rest comes, surely one may drop it for a time?"

"Do you feel like that?" she remarked indifferently. "For myself, during these days I have but one thought. There is nothing else in my life. And you, with all those thousands and millions of your fellow creatures toiling, watching and waiting for a sign from you—oh, I can't imagine how your thoughts can ever wander from them for a moment, how you can ever remember that self even exists! I should like to be trusted, Mr. Fenn, as you are trusted."

"My work," he said complacently, "has, I hope, justified that trust."

"Naturally," she assented, "and yet the greatest part of it is to come. Tell me about Mr. Orden?"

"There is no change in the fellow's attitude. I don't imagine there will be until the last moment. He is just a pig-headed, insufferably conceited Englishman, full of class prejudices to his finger tips."

"He is nevertheless a man," she said thoughtfully. "I heard only yesterday that he earned considerable distinction even in his brief soldiering."

"No doubt," Fenn remarked, without enthusiasm, "he has the bravery of an animal. By the bye, the Bishop dropped in to see me this morning."

"Really?" she asked. "What did he want?"

"Just a personal call," was the elaborately careless reply. "He likes to look in for a chat, now and then. He spoke about Orden, too. I persuaded him that if we don't succeed within the next twenty four hours, it will be his duty to see what he can do."

"Oh, but that was too bad!" she declared. "You know how he feels his position, poor man. He will simply loathe having to tell Julian— Mr. Orden, I mean that he is connected with—"

"Well, with what, Miss Abbeway?"

"With anything in the nature of a conspiracy. Of course, Mr. Orden wouldn't understand. How could he? I think it was cruel to bring the Bishop into the matter at all."

"Nothing," Fenn pronounced, "is cruel that helps the cause. What will you drink, Miss Abbeway? You'll have some champagne, won't you?"

"What a horrible idea!" she exclaimed, smiling at him nevertheless. "Fancy a great Labour leader suggesting such a thing! No, I'll have some light French wine, thank you."

Fenn passed the order on to the waiter, a little crestfallen.

"I don't often drink anything myself," he said, "but this seemed to me to be something of an occasion."

"You have some news, then?"

"Not at all. I meant dining with you."

She raised her eyebrows.

"Oh, that?" she murmured. "That is simply a matter of routine. I thought you had some news, or some work."

"Isn't it possible, Miss Abbeway," he pleaded, "that we might have some interests outside our work?"

"I shouldn't think so," she answered, with an insolence which was above his head.

"There is no reason why we shouldn't have," he persisted.

"You must tell me your tastes," she suggested. "Are you fond of grand opera, for instance? I adore it. 'Parsifal'—'The Ring'?"

"I don't know much about music," he admitted. "My sister, who used to live with me, plays the piano."

"We'll drop music, then," she said hastily. "Books? But I remember you once told me that you had never read anything except detective novels, and that you didn't care for poetry. Sports? I adore tennis and I am rather good at golf."

"I have never wasted a single moment of my life in games," he declared proudly.

She shrugged her shoulders.

"Well, you see, that leaves us rather a long way apart, outside our work, doesn't it?"

"Even if I were prepared to admit that, which I am not," he replied, "our work itself is surely enough to make up for all other things."

"You are quite right," she confessed. "There is nothing else worth thinking about, worth talking about. Tell me—you had an inner Council this afternoon—is anything decided yet about the leadership?"

He sighed a little.

"If ever there was a great cause in the world," he said, "which stands some chance of missing complete success through senseless and low-minded jealousy, it is ours."

"Mr. Fenn!" she exclaimed.

"I mean it," he assured her. "As you know, a chairman must be elected this week, and that chairman, of course, will hold more power in his hand than any emperor of the past or any sovereign of the present. That leader is going to stop the war. He is going to bring peace to the world. It is a mighty post, Miss Abbeway."

"It is indeed," she agreed.

"Yet would you believe," he went on, leaning across the table and neglecting for a moment his dinner, "would you believe, Miss Abbeway, that out of the twenty representatives chosen from the Trades Unions governing the principal industries of Great Britain, there is not a single one who does not consider himself eligible for the post."

Catherine found herself suddenly laughing, while Fenn looked at her in astonishment.

"I cannot help it," she apologised. "Please forgive me. Do not think that I am irreverent. It is not that at all. But for a moment the absurdity of the thing overcame me. I have met some of them, you know— Mr. Cross of Northumberland, Mr. Evans of South Wales—"

"Evans is one of the worst," Fenn interrupted, with some excitement. "There's a man who has only worn a collar for the last few years of his life, who evaded the board-school because he was a pitman's lad, who doesn't even know the names of the countries of Europe, but who still believes that he is a possible candidate. And Cross, too! Well, he washes when he comes to London, but he sleeps in his clothes and they look like it."

"He is very eloquent," Catherine observed.

"Eloquent!" Fenn exclaimed scornfully. "He may be, but who can understand him? He speaks in broad Northumbrian. What is needed in the leader whom they are to elect this week, Miss Abbeway, is a man of some culture and some appearance. Remember that to him is to be confided the greatest task ever given to man. A certain amount of personality he must have—personality and dignity, I should say, to uphold the position."

"There is Mr. Miles Furley," she said thoughtfully. "He is an educated man, is he not?"

"For that very reason unsuitable," Fenn explained eagerly. "He represents no great body of toilers. He is, in reality, only an honorary member of the Council, like yourself and the Bishop, there on account of his outside services."

"I remember, only a few nights ago," she reflected, "I was staying at a country house—Lord Maltenby's, by the bye—Mr. Orden's father. The Prime Minister was there and another Cabinet Minister. They spoke of the Labour Party and its leaderless state. They had no idea, of course, of the great Council which was already secretly formed, but they were unanimous about the necessity for a strong leader. Two people made the same remark, almost with apprehension: 'If ever Paul Fiske should materialise, the problem would be solved!'"

Fenn assented without enthusiasm.

"After all, though," he reminded her, "a clever writer does not always make a great speaker, nor has he always that personality and distinction which is required in this case. He would come amongst us a stranger, too—a stranger personally, that is to say."

"Not in the broadest sense of the word," Catherine objected. "Paul Fiske is more than an ordinary literary man. His heart is in tune with what he writes. Those are not merely eloquent words which he offers. There is a note of something above and beyond just phrase-making—a note of sympathetic understanding which amounts to genius."

Her companion stroked his moustache for a moment.

"Fiske goes right to the spot," he admitted, "but the question of the leadership, so far as he is concerned, doesn't come into the sphere of practical politics. It has been suggested, Miss Abbeway, by one or two of the more influential delegates, suggested, too, by a vast number of letters and telegrams which have poured in upon us during the last few days, that I should be elected to this vacant post."

"You?" she exclaimed, a little blankly.

"Can you think of a more suitable person?" he asked, with a faint note of truculence in his tone. "You have seen us all together. I don't wish to flatter myself, but as regards education, service to the cause, familiarity with public speaking and the number of those I represent—"

"Yes, yes! I see," she interrupted. "Taking the twenty Labour representatives only, Mr. Fenn, I can see nothing against your selection, but I fancied, somehow, that some one outside—the Bishop, for instance—"

"Absolutely out of the question," Fenn declared. "The people would lose faith in the whole thing in a minute. The person who throws down the gage to the Prime Minister must have the direct mandate of the people."

They finished dinner presently. Fenn looked with admiration at the gold, coroneted case from which Catherine helped herself to one of her tiny cigarettes. He himself lit an American cigarette.

"I had meant, Miss Abbeway," he confided, leaning towards her, "to suggest a theatre to you to-night—in fact, I looked at some dress circle seats at the Gaiety with a view to purchasing. Another matter has cropped up, however. There is a little business for us to do."

"Business?" Catherine repeated.

He produced a folded paper from his pocket and passed it across the table. Catherine read it with a slight frown.

"An order entitling the bearer to search Julian Orden's apartments!" she exclaimed. "We don't want to search them, do we? Besides, what authority have we?"

"The best," he answered, tapping with his discoloured forefinger the signature at the foot of the strip of paper.

She examined it with a doubtful frown.

"But how did this come into your possession?" she asked.

He smiled at her in superior fashion.

"By asking for it," he replied bluntly. "And between you and me, Miss Abbeway, there isn't much we might ask for that they'd care to refuse us just now."

"But the police have already searched Mr. Orden's rooms," she reminded him.

"The police have been known to overlook things. Of course, what I am hoping is that amongst Mr. Orden's papers there may be some indication as to where he has deposited our property."

"But this has nothing to do with me," she protested. "I do not like to be concerned in such affairs."

"But I particularly wish you to accompany me," he urged. "You are the only one who has seen the packet. It would be better, therefore, if we conducted the search in company."

Catherine made a little grimace, but she objected no further. She objected very strongly, however, when Fenn tried to take her arm on leaving the place, and she withdrew into her own corner of the taxi immediately they had taken their seats.

"You must forgive my prejudices, Mr. Fenn," she said—"my foreign bringing up, perhaps—but I hate being touched."

"Oh, come!" he remonstrated. "No need to be so stand-offish."

He tried to hold her hand, an attempt which she skilfully frustrated.

"Really," she insisted earnestly, "this sort of thing does not amuse me. I avoid it even amongst my own friends."

"Am I not a friend?" he demanded.

"So far as regards our work, you certainly are," she admitted. "Outside it, I do not think that we could ever have much to say to one another."

"Why not?" he objected, a little sharply. "We're as close together in our work and aims as any two people could be. Perhaps," he went on, after a moment's hesitation and a careful glance around, "I ought to take you into my confidence as regards my personal position."

"I am not inviting anything of the sort," she observed, with faint but wasted sarcasm.

"You know me, of course," he went on, "only as the late manager of a firm of timber merchants and the present elected representative of the allied Timber and Shipbuilding Trades Unions. What you do not know"—a queer note of triumph stealing into his tone "is that I am a wealthy man."

She raised her eyebrows.

"I imagined," she remarked, "that all Labour leaders were like the Apostles—took no thought for such things."

"One must always keep one's eye on the main chance; Miss Abbeway," he protested, "or how would things be when one came to think of marriage, for instance?"

"Where did your money come from?" she asked bluntly.

Her question was framed simply to direct him from a repulsive subject. His embarrassment, however, afforded her food for future thought.

"I have saved money all my life," he confided eagerly. "An uncle left me a little. Lately I have speculated—successfully. I don't want to dwell on this. I only wanted you to understand that if I chose I could cut a very different figure—that my wife wouldn't have to live in a suburb."

"I really do not see," was the cold response, "how this concerns me in the least."

"You, call yourself a Socialist, don't you, Miss Abbeway?" he demanded. "You're not allowing the fact that you're an aristocrat and that I am a self-made man to weigh with you?"

"The accident of birth counts for nothing," she replied, "you must know that those are my principles—but it sometimes happens that birth and environment give one tastes which it is impossible to ignore. Please do not let us pursue this conversation any further, Mr. Fenn. We have had a very pleasant dinner, for which I thank you—and here we are at Mr. Orden's flat."

Her companion handed her out a little sulkily, and they ascended in the lift to the fifth floor. The door was opened to them by Julian's servant. He recognised Catherine and greeted her respectfully. Fenn produced his authority, which the man accepted without comment.

"No news of your master yet?" Catherine asked him.

"None at all, madam," was the somewhat depressed admission. "I am afraid that something must have happened to him. He was not the kind of gentleman to go away like this and leave no word behind him."

"Still," she advised cheerfully, "I shouldn't despair. More wonderful things have happened than that your master should return home to-morrow or the next day with a perfectly simple explanation of his absence."

"I should be very glad to see him, madam," the man replied, as he backed towards the door. "If I can be of any assistance, perhaps you will ring."

The valet departed, closing the door behind him. Catherine looked around the room into which they had been ushered, with a little frown. It was essentially a man's sitting room, but it was well and tastefully furnished, and she was astonished at the immense number of books, pamphlets and Reviews which crowded the walls and every available space. The Derby desk still stood open, there was a typewriter on a special stand, and a pile of manuscript paper.

"What on earth," she murmured, "could Mr. Orden have wanted with a typewriter! I thought journalism was generally done in the offices of a newspaper—the sort of journalism that he used to undertake."

"Nice little crib, isn't it?" Fenn remarked, glancing around. "Cosy little place, I call it."

Something in the man's expression as he advanced towards her brought all the iciness back to her tone and manner.

"It is a pleasant apartment," she said, "but I am not at all sure that I like being here, and I certainly dislike our errand. It does not seem credible that, if the police have already searched, we should find the packet here."

"The police don't know what to look for," he reminded her. "We do."

There was apparently very little delicacy about Mr. Fenn. He drew a chair to the desk and began to look through a pile of papers, making running comments as he did so.

"Hm! Our friend seems to have been quite a collector of old books. I expect second-hand booksellers found him rather a mark. Some fellow here thanking him for a loan. And here's a tailor's bill. By Jove, Miss Abbeway, just listen to this! 'One dress suit-fourteen guineas!' That's the way these fellows who don't know any better chuck their money about," he added, swinging around in his chair towards her. "The clothes I have on cost me exactly four pounds fifteen cash, and I guarantee his were no better."

Catherine frowned impatiently.

"We did not come here, did we, Mr. Fenn, to discuss Mr. Orden's tailor's bill? I can see no object at all in going through his correspondence in this way. What you have to search for is a packet wrapped up in thin yellow oilskin, with 'Number 17' on the outside in black ink."

"Oh, he might have slipped it in anywhere," Fenn pointed out. "Besides, there's always a chance that one of his letters may give us a clue as to where he has hidden the document. Come and sit down by the side of me, won't you, Miss Abbeway? Do!"

"I would rather stand, thank you," she replied. "You seem to find your present occupation to your taste. I should loathe it!"

"Never think of my own feelings," Fenn said briskly, "when there's a job to be done. I wish you'd be a bit more friendly, though, Miss Abbeway. Let me pull that chair up by the side of mine. I like to have you near. You know, I've been a bachelor for a good many years," he went on impressively, "but a little homey place like this always makes me think of things. I've nothing against marriage if only a man can be lucky enough to get the right sort of girl, and although advanced thinkers like you and me and some of the others are looking at things differently, nowadays, I wouldn't mind much which way it was," he confided, dropping his voice a little and laying his hand upon her arm, "if you could make up your mind—"

She snatched her arm away, and this time even he could not mistake the anger which blazed in her eyes.

"Mr. Fenn," she exclaimed, "why is it so difficult to make you understand? I detest such liberties as you are permitting yourself. And for the rest, my affections are already engaged."

"Sounds a bit old-fashioned, that," he remarked, scowling a little. "Of course, I don't expect—"

"Never mind what you expect," she interrupted, "Please go on with this search, if you are going to make one at all. The vulgarity of the whole thing annoys me, and I do not for a moment suppose that the packet is here."

"It wasn't on Orden," he reminded her sullenly.

"Then he must have sent it somewhere for safe keeping," she replied. "I had already given him cause to do so."

"If he has, then amongst his correspondence there may be some indication as to where he sent it," Fenn pointed out, with unabated ill-temper. "If you don't like the job, and you won't be friendly, you'd better take the easy-chair and wait till I'm through."

She sat down, watching him with angry eyes, uncomfortable, unhappy, humiliated. She seemed to have dropped in a few hours from the realms of rarefied and splendid thought to a world of petty deeds. Not one of her companion's actions was lost upon her. She watched him study with ill-concealed reverence a ducal invitation, saw him read through without hesitation a letter which she felt sure was from Julian's mother. And then:

The change in the man was so startling, his muttered exclamation—so natural that its profanity never even grated. His eyes seemed to be starting out of his head, his lips were drawn back from his teeth. Blank, unutterable surprise held him, dumb and spellbound, as he stared at a half-sheet of type written notepaper. She herself, amazed at his transformed appearance, found words for the moment impossible. Then a queer change came into his expression. His eyebrows drew closer together, his lips turned malevolently. He pushed the paper underneath a pile of others and turned his head towards her. Their eyes met. There was something like fear in his.

"What is it that you have found?" she cried breathlessly.

"Nothing," he answered, "nothing of any importance."

She rose slowly to her feet and came towards him.

"I am your partner in this hateful enterprise," she reminded him. "Show me that paper which you have just concealed."

He laid his hand on the lid of the desk, but she caught it and held it open.

"I insist upon seeing it," she said firmly.

He turned and faced her. There was a most unpleasant light in his eyes.

"And I say that you shall not," he declared.

There was a brief, intense silence. Each seemed to be measuring the other's strength. Of the two, Catherine was the more composed. Fenn's face was still white and strained. His lips were twitching, his manner nervous and jerky. He made a desperate effort to reestablish ordinary relations.

"Look here, Miss Abbeway," he said, "we don't need to quarrel about this. That paper I came across has a special interest for me personally. I want to think about it before I say anything to a soul in the world."

"You can consult with me," she persisted. "Our aims are the same. We are here for the same purpose."

"Not altogether," he objected. "I brought you here as my assistant."

"Did you?"

"Well, have the truth, then!" he exclaimed. "I brought you here to be alone with you, because I hoped that I might find you a little kinder."

"I am afraid you have been disappointed, haven't you?" she asked sweetly.

"I have," he answered, with unpleasant meaning in his tone, "but we are not out of here yet."

"You cannot frighten me," she assured him. "Of course, you are a man—of a sort—and I am a woman, but I do not fancy that you would find, if it came to force, that you would have much of an advantage. However, we are wandering from the point. I claim an equal right with you to see anything which you may discover in Mr. Orden's papers. I might, indeed, if I chose, claim a prior right."

"Indeed?" he answered, with an ugly scowl on his face. "Mr. Julian Orden is by way of being a particular friend, eh?"

"As a matter of fact," Catherine told him, "we are engaged to be married. It isn't a serious engagement. It was entered into by him in a most chivalrous manner, to save me from the consequences of a very clumsy attempt on my part to get back that packet. But there it is. Every one down at his home believes at the present moment that we are engaged and that I have come up to London to see our Ambassador."

"If you are engaged," Fenn sneered, "why hasn't he told you more of his secrets?"

"Secrets!" she repeated, a little scornfully. "I shouldn't think he has any. I should imagine his daily life could be investigated without the least fear."

"You'd imagine wrong, then."

"But how interesting! You excite my curiosity. And must you continue to hold my wrist?"

"Let me pull down the top of this desk, then."

"No!"

"Why not?"

"I intend to examine those papers."

With a quick movement he gained a momentary advantage and shut the desk down. The key, however, disturbed by the jerk, fell on to the carpet, and Catherine possessed herself of it. She sprang lightly back from him and pressed the bell.

"D——n you, what are you going to do now?" he demanded.

"You will see," she replied. "Don't come any nearer, or you may find that I can be unpleasant."

He shrugged his shoulders and waited. She turned towards the servant who presently appeared.

"Robert," she said, "will you telephone for me?"

"Certainly, madam," the man answered.

"Telephone to 1884 Westminster. Say that you are speaking for Miss Abbeway, and ask Mr. Furley, Mr. Cross, or whoever is there, to come at once to this address."

"Look here, there's no sense in that," Fenn interrupted.

"Will you do as I ask, please, Robert?" she persisted.

The man bowed and left the room. Fenn strode sulkily back to the desk.

"Very well, then," he conceded, "I give in. Give me the key, and I'll show you the letter."

"You intend to keep your word?"

"I do," he assured her.

She held out the key. He took it, opened the desk, searched amongst the little pile of papers, drew out the half-sheet of notepaper, and handed it to her.

"There you are," he said, "although if you are really engaged to marry Mr. Julian Orden," he added, with disagreeable emphasis, "I am surprised that he should have kept such a secret from you."

She ignored him and started to read the letter, glancing first at the address at the top. It was from the British Review, and was dated a few days back:

> My dear Orden,
>
> I think it best to let you know, in case you haven't seen it yourself, that there is a reward of 100 pounds offered by some busybody for the name of the author of the 'Paul Fiske' articles. Your anonymity has been splendidly preserved up till now, but I feel compelled to warn you that a disclosure is imminent. Take my advice and accept it with a good grace. You have established yourself so irrevocably now that the value of your work will not be lessened by the discovery of the fact that you yourself do not belong to the class of whom you have written so brilliantly.
>
> I hope to see you in a few days.
>
> > Sincerely,
> > M. HALKIN

Even after she had concluded the letter, she still stared at it. She read again the one conclusive sentence—"Your anonymity has been splendidly preserved up till now." Then she suddenly broke into a laugh which was almost hysterical.

"So this is his hack journalism!" she exclaimed. "Julian Orden—Paul Fiske!"

"I don't wonder you're surprised," Fenn observed. "Fourteen guineas for a dress suit, and he thinks he understands the working man!"

She turned her head slowly and looked at him. There was a strange, repressed fire in her eyes. "You are a very foolish person," she said. "Your parents, I suppose, were small shopkeepers, or something of the sort, and you were brought up at a board-school and Julian Orden at Eton and Oxford, and yet he understands, and you do not. You see, heart counts, and sympathy, and the flair for understanding. I doubt whether these things are really found where you come from."

He caught up his hat. His face was very white. His tone shook with anger.

"This is our own fault," he exclaimed angrily, "for having ever permitted an aristocrat to hold any place in our counsels! Before we move a step further, we'll purge them of such helpers as you and such false friends as Julian Orden."

"You very foolish person," she repeated. "Stop, though. Why all this mystery? Why did you try to keep that letter from me?"

"I conceived it to be for the benefit of our cause," he said didactically, "that the anonymity—of 'Paul Fiske' should be preserved."

"Rubbish!" she scoffed. "You were afraid of him. Why, what fools we are! We will tell him the whole truth. We will tell him of our great scheme. We will tell him what we have been working for, these many months. The Bishop shall tell him, and you and I, and Miles Furley, and Cross. He shall hear all about it. He is with us! He must be with us! You shall put him on the Council. Why, there is your great difficulty solved," she went on, in growing excitement. "There is not a working man in the country who would not rally under 'Paul Fiske's' banner. There you have your leader. It is he who shall deliver your ultimatum."

"I'm damned if it is!" Fenn declared, suddenly throwing his hat down and coming towards her furiously. "I'm—"

The door opened. Robert stood there.

"The message, madam," he began—and then stopped short. She crossed the room towards him.

"Robert," she said, "I think I have found the way to bring your master back to you. Will you take me downstairs, please, and fetch me a taxi?"

"Certainly, madam!"

She looked back from the threshold.

"I shall telephone to Westminster in a few minutes, Mr. Fenn," she said. "I hope I shall be in time to stop the others from coming. Perhaps you had better wait here, in case they have already started."

He made no reply. To Catherine the world had become so wonderful that his existence scarcely counted.

XII

Catherine, notwithstanding her own excitement, found genuine pleasure in the bewildered enthusiasm with which the Bishop received her astounding news. She found him alone in the great, gloomy house which he usually inhabited when in London, at work in a dreary library to which she was admitted after a few minutes' delay. Naturally, he received her tidings at first almost with incredulity. A heartfelt joy, however, followed upon conviction.

"I always liked Julian," he declared. "I always believed that he had capacity. Dear me, though," he went on, with a whimsical little smile, "what a blow for the Earl!"

Catherine laughed.

"Do you remember the evening we all talked about the Labour question? Time seems to have moved so rapidly lately, but it was scarcely a week ago."

"I remember," the Bishop acknowledged. "And, my dear young lady," he went on warmly, "now indeed I feel that I can offer you congratulations which come from my heart."

She turned a little away.

"Don't," she begged. "You would have known very soon, in any case— my engagement to Julian Orden was only a pretence."

"A pretence?"

"I was desperate," she explained. "I felt I must have that packet back at any price. I went to his rooms to try and steal it. Well, I was found there. He invented our engagement to help me out."

"But you went off to London together, the neat day?" the Bishop reminded her.

"It was all part of the game," she sighed. "What a fool he must have thought me! However, I am glad. I am riotously, madly glad. I am glad for the cause, I am glad for all our sakes. We have a great recruit, Bishop, the greatest we could have. And think! When he knows the truth, there will be no more trouble. He will hand us over the packet. We shall know just where we stand. We shall know at once whether we dare to strike the great blow."

"I was down at Westminster this afternoon," the Bishop told her. "The whole mechanism of the Council of Labour seems to be complete. Twenty men control industrial England. They have absolute power. They are waiting only for the missing word. And fancy," he went on, "to-morrow I was to have visited Julian. I was to have used my persuasions."

"But we must go to-night!" Catherine exclaimed. "There is no reason why we should waste a single second."

"I shall be only too pleased," he assented gladly. "Where is, he?"

Catherine's face fell.

"I haven't the least idea," she confessed. "Don't you know?"

The Bishop shook his head.

"They were going to send some one with me tomorrow," he replied, "but in any case Fenn knows. We can get at him."

She made a little wry face.

"I do not like Mr. Fenn," she said slowly. "I have disagreed with him. But that does not matter. Perhaps we had better go to the Council rooms. We shall find some of them there, and probably Fenn. I have a taxi waiting."

They drove presently to Westminster. The ground floor of the great building, which was wholly occupied now by the offices of the different Labour men, was mostly in darkness, but on the top floor was a big room used as a club and restaurant, and also for informal meetings. Six or seven of the twenty-three were there, but not Fenn. Cross, a great brawny Northumbrian, was playing a game of chess with Furley. Others were writing letters. They all turned around at Catherine's entrance. She held out her hands to them.

"Great news, my friends!" she exclaimed. "Light up the committee room. I want to talk to you."

Those who were entitled to followed her into the room across the passage. One or two secretaries and a visitor remained outside. Six of them seated themselves at the long table—Phineas Cross, the Northumbrian pitman, Miles Furley, David Sands, representative of a million Yorkshire mill-hands, Thomas Evans, the South Wales miner.

"We got a message from you, Miss Abbeway, a little time ago," Furley remarked. "It was countermanded, though, just as we were ready to start."

"Yes!" she assented. "I am sorry. I telephoned from Julian Orden's rooms. It was there we made the great discovery. Listen, all of you! I have discovered the identity of Paul Fiske."

There was a little clamour of voices. The interest was indescribable. Paul Fiske was their cult, their master, their undeniable prophet. It was he who had set down in letters of fire the truths which had been struggling for imperfect expression in these men's minds. It was Paul

Fiske who had fired them with enthusiasm for the cause which at first had been very much like a matter of bread and cheese to them. It was Paul Fiske who had formed their minds, who had put the great arguments into their brains, who had armed them from head to foot with potent reasonings. Four very ordinary men, of varying types, sincere men, all of plebeian extraction, all with their faults, yet all united in one purpose, were animated by that same fire of excitement. They hung over the table towards her. She might have been the croupier and they the gamblers who had thrown upon the table their last stake.

"In Julian Orden's rooms," she said, "I found a letter from the editor of the British Review, warning him that his anonymity could not be preserved much longer—that before many weeks had passed the world would know that he was Paul Fiske. Here is the letter."

She passed it around. They studied it, one by one. They were all a little stunned.

"Julian!" Furley exclaimed, in blank amazement. "Why, he's been pulling my leg for more than a year!"

"The son of an Earl!" Cross gasped.

"Never mind about that. He is a democrat and honest to the backbone," Catherine declared. "The Bishop will tell you so. He has known him all his life. Think! Julian Orden has no purpose to serve, no selfish interest to further. He has nothing to gain, everything to lose. If he were not sincere, if those words of his, which we all remember, did not come from his heart, where could be the excuse, the reason, for what he stands for? Think what it means to us!"

"He is the man, isn't he," Sands asked mysteriously, "whom they are looking after down yonder?"

"I don't know where 'down yonder' is," Catherine replied, "but you have him in your power somewhere. He left his rooms last Thursday at about a quarter past six, to take that packet to the Foreign Office, or to make arrangements for its being received there. He never reached the Foreign Office. He hasn't been heard of since. Some of you know where he is. The Bishop and I want to go and find him at once."

"Fenn and Bright know," Cross declared. "It's Bright's job."

"Why is Bright in it?" Catherine asked impatiently.

Cross frowned and puckered up his lips, an odd trick of his when he was displeased.

"Bright represents the workers in chemical factories," he explained. "They say that there isn't a poison in liquid, solid or gas form, that he doesn't know all about. Chap who gives me kind of shivers whenever he comes near. He and Fenn run the secret service branch of the Council."

"If he knows where Mr. Orden is, couldn't we send for him at once?" Catherine suggested.

"I'll go," Furley volunteered.

He was back in a few minutes.

"Fenn and Bright are both out," he announced, "and their rooms locked up. I rang up Fenn's house, but he hasn't been back."

Catherine stamped her foot. She was on fire with impatience.

"Doesn't it seem too bad!" she exclaimed. "If we could only get hold of Julian Orden to-night, if the Bishop and I could talk to him for five minutes, we could have this message for which we have been waiting so long."

The door was suddenly opened. Fenn entered and received a little chorus of welcome. He was wearing a rough black overcoat over his evening clothes, and a black bowler hat. He advanced to the table with a little familiar swagger.

"Mr. Fenn," the Bishop said, "we have been awaiting your arrival anxiously. Tell us, please, where we can find Mr. Julian Orden."

Fenn gave vent to a half-choked, ironical laugh.

"If you'd asked me an hour ago," he said, "I should have told you to try Iris Villa, Acacia Road, Hampstead. I have just come from there."

"You saw him?" the Bishop enquired.

"That's just what I did not," Fenn replied.

"Why not?" Catherine demanded.

"Because he wasn't there, hasn't been since three o'clock this afternoon."

"You've moved him?" Furley asked eagerly.

"He's moved himself," was the grim reply. "He's escaped."

During the brief, spellbound silence which followed his announcement, Fenn advanced slowly into the room. It chanced that during their informal discussion, the chair at the head of the table had been left unoccupied. The newcomer hesitated for a single second, then removed his hat, laid it on the floor by his side, and sank into the vacant seat. He glanced somewhat defiantly towards Catherine. He seemed to know quite well from whence the challenge of his words would come.

"You tell us," Catherine said, mastering her emotion with an effort, "that Julian Orden, whom we now know to be 'Paul Fiske', has escaped. Just what do you mean?"

E. PHILLIPS OPPENHEIM

"I can scarcely reduce my statement to plainer words," Fenn replied, "but I will try. The danger in which we stood through the miscarriage of that packet was appreciated by every one of the Council. Discretionary powers were handed to the small secret service branch which is controlled by Bright and myself. Orden was prevented from reaching the Foreign Office and was rendered for a time incapable. The consideration of our further action with regard to him was to depend upon his attitude. Owing, no doubt, to some slight error in Bright's treatment. Orden has escaped from the place of safety in which he had been placed. He is now at large, and his story, together with the packet, will probably be in the hands of the Foreign Office some time to-night."

"Giving them," Cross remarked grimly, "the chance to get in the first blow—warrants for high treason, eh, against the twenty-three of us?"

"I don't fear that," Fenn asserted, "not if we behave like sensible men. My proposal is that we anticipate, that one of us sees the Prime Minister to-morrow morning and lays the whole position before him."

"Without the terms," Furley observed.

"I know exactly what they will be," Fenn pointed out. "The trouble, of course, is that the missing packet contains the signature of the three guarantors. The packet, no doubt, will be in the hands of the Foreign Office by to-morrow. The Prime Minister can verify our statements. We present our ultimatum a little sooner than we intended, but we get our blow in first and we are ready."

The Bishop leaned forward in his place.

"Forgive me if I intervene for one moment," he begged. "You say that Julian Orden has escaped. Are we to understand that he is absolutely at liberty and in a normal state of health?"

Fenn hesitated for a single second.

"I have no reason to believe the contrary," he said.

"Still, it is possible," the Bishop persisted, "that Julian Orden may not be in a position to forward that document to the Foreign Office for the present? If that is so, I am inclined to think that the Prime Minister would consider your visit a bluff. Certainly, you would have no argument weighty enough to induce him to propose the armistice. No man could act upon your word alone. He would want to see these wonderful proposals in writing, even if he were convinced of the justice of your arguments."

There was a little murmur of approval. Fenn leaned forward.

"You drive me to a further disclosure," he declared, after a moment's hesitation, "one, perhaps, which I ought already to have made. I have arranged for a duplicate of that packet to be prepared and forwarded. I set this matter on foot the moment we heard from Miss Abbeway here of her mishap. The duplicate may reach us at any moment."

"Then I propose," the Bishop said, "that we postpone our decision until those papers be received. Remember that up to the present moment the Council have not pledged themselves to take action until they have perused that document."

"And supposing," Fenn objected, "that to-morrow morning at eight o'clock, twenty-three of us are marched off to the Tower! Our whole cause may be paralysed, all that we have worked for all these months will be in vain, and this accursed and bloody war may be dragged on until our politicians see fit to make a peace of words."

"I know Mr. Stenson well," the Bishop declared, "and I am perfectly convinced that he is too sane-minded a man to dream of taking such a step as you suggest. He, at any rate, if others in his Cabinet are not so prescient, knows what Labour means."

"I agree with the Bishop, for many reasons," Furley pronounced.

"And I," Cross echoed.

The sense of the meeting was obvious. Fenn's unpleasant looking teeth flashed for a moment, and his mouth came together with a little snap.

"This is entirely an informal gathering," he said. "I shall summon the Council to come together tomorrow at midday."

"I think that we may sleep in our beds to-night without fear of molestation," the Bishop remarked, "although if it had been the wish of the meeting, I would have broached the matter to Mr. Stenson."

"You are an honorary member of the Council," Fenn declared rudely. "We don't wish interference. This is a national and international Labour movement."

"I am a member of the Labour Party of Christ," the Bishop said quietly.

"And an honoured member of this Executive Council," Cross intervened. "You're a bit too glib with your tongue to-night, Fenn."

"I think of those whom I represent," was the curt reply. "They are toilers, and they want the toilers to show their power. They don't want help from the Church. I'll go even so far," he added, "as to say that they don't want help from literature. It's their own job. They've begun it, and they want to finish it."

"To-morrow's meeting," Furley observed, "will show how far you are right in your views. I consider my position, and the Bishop's, as members of the Labour Party, on a par with your own. I will go further and say that the very soul of our Council is embodied in the teachings and the writings of Paul Fiske, or, as we now know him to be, Julian Orden."

Fenn rose to his feet. He was trembling with passion.

"This informal meeting is adjourned," he announced harshly.

Cross himself did not move.

"Adjourned or not it may be, Mr. Fenn," he said, "but it's no place of yours to speak for it. You've thrust yourself into that chair, but that don't make you chairman, now or at any other time."

Fenn choked down the words which had seemed to tremble on his lips. His enemies he knew, but there were others here who might yet be neutral.

"If I have assumed more than I should have done, I am sorry," he said. "I brought you news which I was in a hurry to deliver. The rest followed."

The little company rose to their feet and moved towards the door, exchanging whispered comments concerning the news which Catherine had brought. She herself crossed the room and confronted Fenn.

"There is still something to be said about that news," she declared.

Fenn's attempt at complete candour was only partially convincing.

"There is not the slightest reason," he declared, "why anything concerning Julian Orden should be concealed from any member of the Council who desires information. If you will follow me into my private room, Miss Abbeway, and you, Furley, I shall be glad to tell you our exact position. And if the Bishop will accompany you," he added, turning to the latter, "I shall be honoured."

Furley made no reply, but, whispering something in Catherine's ear, took up his hat and left the room. The other two, however, took Fenn at his word, followed him into his room, accepted the chairs which he placed for them, and waited while he spoke through a telephone to the private exchange situated in the building.

"They tell me," he announced, as he laid down the instrument, "that Bright has this moment returned and is now on his way upstairs."

Catherine shivered.

"Is Mr. Bright that awful-looking person who came to the last Council meeting?"

"He is probably the person you mean," Fenn assented. "He takes very little interest in our executive work, but he is one of the most brilliant scientists of this or any other generation. The Government has already given him three laboratories for his experiments, and nearly every gas that is being used at the Front has been prepared according to his formula."

"A master of horrors," the Bishop murmured.

"He looks it," Catherine whispered under her breath.

There was a knock at the door, a moment or two later, and Bright entered. He was a little over medium height, with long and lanky figure, a pronounced stoop, and black, curly hair of coarse quality. His head, which was thrust a little forward, perhaps owing to his short-sightedness, was long, his forehead narrow, his complexion a sort of olive-green. He wore huge, disfiguring spectacles, and he had the protuberant lips of a negro. He greeted Catherine and the Bishop absently and seemed to have a grievance against Fenn.

"What is it you want, Nicholas?" he asked impatiently. "I have some experiments going on in the country and can only spare a minute."

"The Council has rescinded its instructions with regard to Julian Orden," Fenn announced, "and is anxious to have him brought before them at once. As you know, we are for the moment powerless in the matter. Will you please explain to Miss Abbeway and the Bishop here just what has been done?"

"It seems a waste of time," Bright replied ill-naturedly, "but here is the story. Julian Orden left his rooms at a quarter to six on Thursday evening. He walked down to St. James's Street and turned into the Park. Just as he passed the side door of Marlborough House he was attacked by a sudden faintness."

"For which, I suppose," the Bishop interrupted, "you were responsible."

"I or my deputy," Bright replied. "It doesn't matter which. He was fortunate enough to be able to hail a passing taxicab and was driven to my house in Hampstead. He has spent the intervening period, until three o'clock this afternoon, in a small laboratory attached to the premises."

"A compulsory stay, I presume?" the Bishop ventured.

"A compulsory stay, arranged for under instructions from the Council," Bright assented, in his hard, rasping voice. "He has been most of the time under the influence of some new form of anaesthetic gas with which I have been experimenting. To-night, however, I must have made a mistake in my calculations. Instead of remaining in a state of coma until midnight, he recovered during my absence and appears to have walked out of the place."

"You have no idea where he is at the present moment, then?" Catherine asked.

"Not the slightest," Bright assured her. "I only know that he left the place without hat, gloves, or walking stick. Otherwise, he was fully dressed, and no doubt had plenty of money in his pocket."

"Is he likely to have any return of the indisposition from which, owing to your efforts, he has been suffering?" the Bishop enquired.

"I should say not," was the curt answer. "He may find his memory somewhat affected temporarily. He ought to be able to find his way home, though. If not, I suppose you'll hear of him through the police courts or a hospital. Nothing that we have done," he added, after a moment's pause, "is likely to affect his health permanently in the slightest degree."

"You now know all that there is to be known, Miss Abbeway," Fenn said. "I agree with you that it is highly desirable that Mr. Orden should be found at once, and if you can suggest any way in which I might be of assistance in discovering his present whereabouts, I shall be only too glad to help. For instance, would you like me to telephone to his rooms?"

Catherine rose to her feet.

"Thank you, Mr. Fenn," she said, "I don't think that we will trouble you. Mr. Furley is making enquiries both at Mr. Orden's rooms and at his clubs."

"You are perfectly satisfied, so far as I am concerned, I trust?" he persisted, as he opened the door for them.

"Perfectly satisfied," Catherine replied, looking him in the face, "that you have told us as much as you choose to for the present."

Fenn closed the door behind Catherine and the Bishop and turned back into the room. Bright laughed at him unpleasantly.

"Love affair not going so strong, eh?"

Fenn threw himself into his chair, took a cigarette from a paper packet, and lit it.

"Blast Julian Orden!" he muttered.

"No objection," his friend yawned. "What's wrong now?"

"Haven't you heard the news? It seems he's the fellow who has been writing those articles on Socialism and Labour, signing them 'Paul Fiske.' Idealistic rubbish, but of course the Bishop and his lot are raving about him."

"I've read some of his stuff," Bright admitted, himself lighting a cigarette; "good in its way, but old-fashioned. I'm out for something a little more than that."

"Stick to the point," Fenn enjoined morosely. "Now they've found out who Julian Orden is, they want him produced. They want to elect him on the Council, make him chairman over all our heads, let him reap the reward of the scheme which our brains have conceived."

"They want him, eh? That's awkward."

"Awkward for us," Fenn muttered.

"They'd better have him, I suppose," Bright said, with slow and evil emphasis. "Yes, they'd better have him. We'll take off our hats, and assure him that it was a mistake."

"Too late. I've told Miss Abbeway and the Bishop that he is at large. You backed me up."

Bright thrust his long, unpleasant, knobby fingers into his pocket, and produced a crumpled cigarette, which he lit from the end of his companion's.

"Well," he demanded, "what do you want?"

"I have come to the conclusion," Fenn decided, "that it is not in the interests of our cause that Orden should become associated with it in any way."

"We've a good deal of power," Bright ruminated, "but it seems to me you're inclined to stretch it. I gather that the others want him delivered up. We can't act against them."

"Not if they know," Fenn answered significantly.

Bright came over to the mantelpiece, leaned his elbow upon it, and hung his extraordinarily unattractive face down towards his companion's.

"Nicholas," he said, "I don't blame you for fencing, but I like plain words. You've done well out of this new Party. I haven't. You've no hobby except saving your money. I have. My last two experiments, notwithstanding the Government allowance, have left me drained. I need money as you others need bread. I can live without food or drink, but I can't be without the means to keep my laboratories going. Do you understand me?"

"I do," Fenn assented, taking up his hat. "Come, I'll drive towards Bermondsey with you. We'll talk on the way."

E. PHILLIPS OPPENHEIM

XIII

Julian raised himself slightly from his recumbent position at the sound of the opening of the door. He watched Fenn with dull, incurious eyes as the latter crossed the uncarpeted floor of the bare wooden shed, threw off his overcoat, and advanced towards the side of the couch.

"Sit up a little," the newcomer directed.

Julian shook his head.

"No strength," he muttered. "If I had, I should wring your damned neck!"

Fenn looked down at him for a moment in silence.

"You take this thing very hardly, Mr. Orden," he said. "I think that you had better give up this obstinacy. Your friends are getting anxious about you. For many reasons it would be better for you to reappear."

"There will be a little anxiety on the part of your friends about you," Julian retorted grimly, "if ever I do get out of this accursed place."

"You bear malice, I fear, Mr. Orden."

Julian made no reply. His eyes were fixed upon the door. He turned away with a shudder. Bright had entered. In his hand he was carrying two gas masks. He came over to the side of the couch, and, looking down at Julian, lifted his hand, and felt his pulse. Then, with an abrupt movement, he handed one of the masks to Fenn.

"Look out for yourself," he advised. "I am going to give him an antidote."

Bright stepped back and adjusted his own gas mask, while Fenn followed suit. Then the former drew from his pocket what seemed to be a small tube with perforated holes at the top. He leaned over Julian and pressed it. A little cloud of faint mist rushed through the holes; a queer, aromatic perfume, growing stronger every moment, seemed to creep into the farthest corners of the room. In less than ten seconds Julian opened his eyes. In half a minute he was sitting up. His eyes were bright once more, there was colour in his cheeks. Bright spoke to him warningly.

"Mr. Orden," he enjoined, "sit where you are. Remember I have the other tube in my left hand."

"You infernal scoundrel!" Julian exclaimed.

"Mr. Bright," Fenn asserted, "is nothing of the sort. Neither am I. We are both honest men faced with a colossal situation. There is nothing personal in our treatment of you. We have no enmity towards you. You are simply a person who has committed a theft."

"What puzzles me," Julian muttered, "is what you expect I am going to do about you, if ever I do escape from your clutches."

"If you do escape," Fenn said quietly, "you will view the matter differently. You will find, as a matter of fact, that you are powerless to do anything. You will find a new law and a new order prevailing."

"German law!" Julian sneered.

"You misjudge us," Fenn continued. "Both Bright and I are patriotic Englishmen. We are engaged at the present moment in a desperate effort to save our country. You are the man who stands in the way."

"I never thought," said Julian, "that I should smile in this place, but you are beginning to amuse me. Why not be more explicit? Why not prove what you say? I might become amenable. I suppose your way of saving the country is to hand it over to the Germans, eh?"

"Our way of saving the country," Fenn declared, "is to establish peace."

Julian laughed scornfully.

"I know a little about you, Mr. Fenn," he said. "I know the sort of peace you would establish, the sort of peace any man would propose who conducts a secret correspondence with Germany."

Fenn, who had lifted his mask for a moment, slowly rearranged it.

"Mr. Orden," he said, "we are not going to waste words upon you. You are hopelessly and intolerably prejudiced. Will you tell us where you have concealed the packet you intercepted?"

"Aren't you almost tired of asking me that question? I'm tired of hearing it," Julian replied. "I will not."

"Will you let me try to prove to you," Fenn begged, "that by the retention of that packet you are doing your country an evil service?"

"If you talked till doomsday," Julian assured him, "I should not believe a word you said."

"In that case," Fenn began slowly, with an evil glitter in his eyes!!!!!

"Well, for heaven's sake finish the thing this time!" Julian interrupted. "I'm sick of playing the laboratory rabbit for you. If you are out for murder, finish the job and have done with it."

Bright was playing with another tube which he had withdrawn from his pocket.

"It is my duty to warn you, Mr. Orden," he said, "that the contents of this little tube of gas, which will reach you with a touch of my fingers, may possibly be fatal and will certainly incapacitate you for life."

"Why warn me?" Julian scoffed. "You know very well that I haven't the strength of a cat, or I should wring your neck."

"We feel ourselves," Bright continued unctuously, "justified in using this tube, because its first results will be to throw you into a delirium, in the course of which we trust that you will divulge the hiding place of the stolen packet. We use this means in the interests of the country, and such risk as there may be lies on your own head."

"You're a canting hypocrite!" Julian declared. "Try your delirium. That packet happens to be in the one place where neither you nor one of your tribe could get at it."

"It is a serious moment, this, Mr. Orden," Fenn reminded him. "You are in the prime of life, and there is a scandal connected with your present position which your permanent disappearance would certainly not dissipate. Remember—"

He stopped short. A whistle in the corner of the room was blowing. Bright moved towards it, but at that moment there was the sound of flying footsteps on the wooden stairs outside, and the door was flung open. Catherine, breathless with haste, paused for a moment on the threshold, then came forward with a little cry.

"Julian!" she exclaimed.

He gazed at her, speechless, but with a sudden light in his eyes. She came across the room and dropped on her knees by his couch. The two men fell back. Fenn slipped back between her and the door. They both removed their masks, but they held them ready.

"Oh, how dared they!" she went on. "The beasts! Tell me, are you ill?"

"Weak as a kitten," he faltered. "They've poisoned me with their beastly gases."

Catherine rose to her feet. She faced the two men, her eyes flashing with anger.

"The Council will require an explanation of this, Mr. Fenn!" she declared passionately. "Barely an hour ago you told us that Mr. Orden had escaped from Hampstead."

"Julian Orden," Fenn replied, "has been handed over to our secret service by the unanimous vote of the Council. We have absolute liberty to deal with him as we think fit."

"Have you liberty to tell lies as to his whereabouts?" Catherine demanded. "You deliberately told the Council he had escaped, yet, entirely owing to Mr. Furley, I find you down here at Bermondsey with him. What were you going to do with him when I came in?"

"Persuade him to restore the packet, if we could," Fenn answered sullenly.

"Rubbish!" Catherine retorted. "You know very well that he is our friend. You have only to tell him the truth, and your task with him is at an end."

"Steady!" Julian muttered. "Don't imagine that I have any sympathy with your little nest of conspirators."

"That is only because you do not understand," Catherine assured him. "Listen, and you shall hear the whole truth. I will tell you what is inside that packet and whose signatures you will find there."

Julian gripped her wrist suddenly. His eyes were filled with a new fear. He was watching the two men, who were whispering together.

"Catherine," he exclaimed warningly, "look out! These men mean mischief. That devil Bright invents a new poisonous gas every day. Look at Fenn buckling on his mask. Quick! Get out if you can!"

Catherine's hand touched her bosom. Bright sprang towards her, but he was too late. She raised a little gold whistle to her lips, and its pealing summons rang through the room. Fenn dropped his mask and glanced towards Bright. His face was livid.

"Who's outside?" he demanded.

"The Bishop and Mr. Furley. Great though my confidence is in you both, I scarcely ventured to come here alone."

The approaching footsteps were plainly audible. Fenn shrugged his shoulders with a desperate attempt at carelessness.

"I don't know what is in your mind, Miss Abbeway," he said. "You can scarcely believe that you, at any rate, were in danger at our hands."

"I would not trust you a yard," she replied fiercely. "In any case, it is better that the others should come. Mr. Orden might not believe me. He will at least believe the Bishop."

"Believe whom?" Julian demanded.

The door was opened. The Bishop and Miles Furley came hastily in. Catherine stepped forward to meet them.

"I was obliged to whistle," she explained, a little hysterically. "I do not trust either of these men. That fiend Bright has a poisonous gas with him in a pocket cylinder. I am convinced that they meant to murder Julian."

The two newcomers turned towards the couch and exchanged amazed greetings with Julian. Fenn threw his mask on to the table with an uneasy laugh.

"Miss Abbeway," he protested, "is inclined to be melodramatic. The gas which Bright has in that cylinder is simply one which would produce a little temporary unconsciousness. We might have used it—we may still use it—but if you others are able to persuade Mr. Orden to restore the packet, our task with him is at an end. We are not his gaolers—or perhaps he would say his torturers—for pleasure. The Council has ordered that we should extort from him the papers you know of and has given us carte blanche as to the means. If you others can persuade him to restore them peaceably, why, do it. We are prepared to wait."

Julian was still staring from one to the other of his visitors. His expression of blank astonishment had scarcely decreased.

"Bishop," he said at last, "unless you want to see me go insane before your eyes, please explain. It can't be possible that you have anything in common with this nest of conspirators."

The Bishop smiled a little wanly. He laid his hand upon his godson's shoulder.

"Believe me, I have been no party to your incarceration, Julian," he declared, "but if you will listen to me, I will tell you why I think it would be better for you to restore that packet to Miss Abbeway."

"Tell that blackguard to give me another sniff of his restorative gas," Julian begged. "These shocks are almost too much for me."

The Bishop turned interrogatively towards Bright, who once more leaned over Julian with the tube in his hand. Again the little mist, the pungent odour. Julian rose to his feet and sat down again.

"I am listening," he said.

"First of all," began the Bishop earnestly, as he seated himself at the end of the couch on which Julian had been lying, "let me try to remove some of your misconceptions. Miss Abbeway is in no sense of the word a German spy. She and I, Mr. Furley here, Mr. Fenn and Mr. Bright, all belong to an organisation leagued together for one purpose—we are determined to end the war."

"Pacifists!" Julian muttered.

"An idle word," the Bishop protested, "because at heart we are all pacifists. There is not one of us who would wilfully choose war instead of peace. The only question is the price we are prepared to pay."

"Why not leave that to the Government?"

"The Government," the Bishop replied, "are the agents of the people. The people in this case wish to deal direct."

"Again why?" Julian demanded.

"Because the Government is composed wholly of politicians, politicians who, in far too many speeches, have pledged themselves to too many definite things. Still, the Government will have its chance."

"Explain to me," Julian asked, "why, if you are a patriotic society, you are in secret and illegal communication with Germany?"

"The Germany with whom we are in communication," the Bishop assured his questioner, "is the Germany who thinks as we do."

"Then you are on a wild-goose chase," Julian declared, "because the Germans who think as you do are in a hopeless minority."

The Bishop's forefinger was thrust out.

"I have you, Julian," he said. "That very belief which you have just expressed is our justification, because it is the common belief throughout the country. I can prove to you that you are mistaken—can prove it, with the help of that very packet which is responsible for your incarceration here."

"Explain," Julian begged.

"That packet," the Bishop declared, "contains the peace terms formulated by the Socialist and Labour parties of Germany."

"Worth precisely the paper it is written on?" Julian scoffed.

"And ratified," the Bishop continued emphatically, "by the three great men of Germany, whose signatures are attached to that document—the Kaiser, the Chancellor and Hindenburg."

Julian was electrified.

"Do you seriously mean," he asked, "that those signatures are attached to proposals of peace formulated by the Socialist and Labour parties of Germany?"

"I do indeed," was the confident reply. "If the terms arc not what we have been led to expect, or if the signatures are not there, the whole affair is at an end."

"You are telling me wonderful things, sir," Julian confessed, after a brief pause.

"I am telling what you will discover yourself to be the truth," the Bishop insisted. "And, Julian, I am appealing to you not only for the return of that packet, but for your sympathy, your help, your partisanship. You can guess now what has happened. Your anonymity has come to an end. The newly formed Council of Labour, to which we all belong, is eager and anxious to welcome you."

"Has any one given me away?" Julian asked.

Catherine shook her head.

"The truth was discovered this evening, when your rooms were searched," she explained.

"What is the constitution of this Council of Labour?" Julian enquired, a little dazed by this revelation.

"It is the very body of men which you yourself foreshadowed," the Bishop replied eagerly. "Twenty of the members are elected by the Trades Unions and represent the great industries of the Empire; and there are three outsiders—Miss Abbeway, Miles Furley and myself. If you, Julian, had not been so successful in concealing your identity, you would have been the first man to whom the Council would have turned for help. Now that the truth is known, your duty is clear. The glory of ending this war will belong to the people, and it is partly owing to you that the people have grown to realise their strength."

"My own position at the present moment," Julian began, a little grimly!!!!!

"You have no one to blame for that but yourself," Catherine interrupted. "If we had known who you were, do you suppose that we should have allowed these men to deal with you in such a manner? Do you suppose that I should not have told you the truth about that packet? However, that is over. You know the truth now. We five are all members of the Council who are sitting practically night and day, waiting—you know what for. Do not keep us in suspense any longer than you can help. Tell us where to find this letter?"

Julian passed his hand over his forehead a little wearily.

"I am confused," he admitted. "I must think. After all, you are engaged in a conspiracy. Stenson's Cabinet may not be the strongest on earth, or the most capable, but Stenson himself has carried the burden of this war bravely."

"If the terms offered," the Bishop pointed out, "are anything like what we expect, they are better than any which the politicians could ever have mooted, even after years more of bloodshed. It is my opinion that Stenson will welcome them, and that the country, generally speaking, will be entirely in favour of their acceptance."

"Supposing," Julian asked, "that you think them reasonable, that you make your demand to the Prime Minister, and he refuses. What then?"

"That," Fenn intervened, with the officious air of one who has been left out of the conversation far too long, "is where we come in. At our word, every coal pit in England would cease work, every furnace fire would go out, every factory would stand empty. The trains would remain on their sidings, or wherever they might chance to be when the edict was pronounced. The same with the 'buses and cabs, the same with the Underground. Not a ship would leave any port in the United Kingdom, not a ship would be docked. Forty-eight hours of this would do more harm than a year's civil war. Forty-eight hours must procure from the Prime Minister absolute submission to our demands. Ours is the greatest power the world has ever evolved. We shall use it for the greatest cause the world has ever known—the cause of peace."

"This, in a way, was inevitable," Julian observed. "You remember the conversation, Bishop," he added, "down at Maltenby?"

"Very well indeed," the latter acquiesced.

"The country went into slavery," Julian pronounced, "in August, 1915. That slavery may or may not be good for them. To be frank, I think it depends entirely upon the constitution of your Council. It is so much to the good, Bishop, that you are there."

"Our Council, such as it is," Fenn remarked acidly, "consists of men elected to their position by the votes of a good many millions of their fellow toilers."

"The people may have chosen wisely," was the grave reply, "or they may have made mistakes. Such things have been known. By the bye, I suppose that my durance is at an end?"

"It is at an end, whichever way you decide," Catherine declared. "Now that you know everything, though, you will not hesitate to give up the packet?"

"You shall have it," he agreed. "I will give it back into your hands."

"The sooner the better!" Fenn exclaimed eagerly. "And, Mr. Orden, one word."

Julian was standing amongst them now, very drawn and pale in the dim halo of light thrown down from the hanging lamp. His answering monosyllable was cold and restrained.

"Well?"

"I trust you will understand," Fenn continued, "that Bright and I were simply carrying out orders. To us you were an enemy. You had betrayed the trust of one of our members. The prompt delivery of that packet meant the salvation of thousands of lives. It meant a cessation of this ghastly world tragedy. We were harsh, perhaps, but we acted according to orders."

Julian glanced at the hand which Fenn had half extended but made no movement to take it. He leaned a little upon the Bishop's arm.

"Help me out of this place, sir, will you?" he begged. "As for Fenn and that other brute, what I have to say about them will keep."

XIV

It was a little more than half an hour later when Julian ascended the steps of his club in Pall Mall and asked the hall porter for letters. Except that he was a little paler than usual and was leaning more heavily upon his stick, there was nothing about his appearance to denote several days of intense strain. There was a shade of curiosity, mingled with surprise, in the commissionaire's respectful greeting.

"There have been a good many enquiries for you the last few days, sir," he observed.

"I dare say," Julian replied. "I was obliged to go out of town unexpectedly."

He ran through the little pile of letters and selected a bulky envelope addressed to himself in his own handwriting. With this he returned to the taxicab in which the Bishop and Catherine were seated. They gazed with fascinated eyes at the packet which he was carrying and which he at once displayed.

"You see," he remarked, as he leaned back, "there is nothing so impenetrable in the world as a club of good standing. It beats combination safes hollow. It would have taken all Scotland Yard to have dragged this letter from the rack."

"That is really—it?" Catherine demanded breathlessly.

"It is the packet," he assured her, "which you handed to me for safe keeping at Maltenby."

They drove almost in silence to the Bishop's house, where it had been arranged that Julian should spend the night. The Bishop left the two together before the fire in his library, while he personally superintended the arrangement of a guest room. Catherine came over and knelt by the side of Julian's chair.

"Shall I beg forgiveness for the past," she whispered, "or may I not talk of the future, the glorious future?"

"Is it to be glorious?" he asked a little doubtfully.

"It can be made so," she answered with fervour, "by you more than by anybody else living. I defy you—you, Paul Fiske—to impugn our scheme, our aims, the goal towards which we strive. All that we needed was a leader who could lift us up above the localness, the narrow visions of these men. They are in deadly earnest, but they can't see far enough, and each sees along his own groove. It is true that at the end the same sun shines, but no assembly of people can move together along a dozen different ways and keep the same goal in view."

He touched the packet.

"We do not yet know the written word here," he reminded her.

"I do," she insisted. "My heart tells me. Besides, I have had many hints. There are people in London whose position forces them to remain silent, who understand and know."

"Foreigners?" Julian asked suspiciously.

"Neutrals, of course, but neutrals of discretion are very useful people. The military party in Germany is making a brave show still, but it is beaten, notwithstanding its victories. The people are gathering together in their millions. Their voice is already being heard. Here we have the proof of it."

"But even if these proposed terms are as favourable as you say," Julian objected, "how can you force them upon the English Cabinet? There is America-France. Yours is purely a home demand. A government has other things to think of and consider."

"France is war-weary to the bone," she declared. "France will follow England, especially when she knows the contents of that packet. As for America, she came into this after the great sacrifices had been made. She demands nothing more than is to be yielded up. It is not for the sake of visionary ideas, not for diplomatic precedence that the humanitarians of the world are going to hesitate about ending this brutal slaughter."

He studied her curiously. In the firelight her face seemed to him almost strangely beautiful. She was uplifted by the fervour of her thoughts. The depth in her soft brown eyes was immeasurable; the quiver of her lips, so soft and yet so spiritual, was almost inspiring. Her hand was resting upon his shoulder. She seemed to dwell upon his expression, to listen eagerly for his words. Yet he realised that in all this there was no personal note. She was the disciple of a holy cause, aflame with purpose.

"It will mean a revolution," he said thoughtfully.

"A revolution was established two years ago," she pointed out, "and the people have held their power ever since. I will tell you what I believe to-day," she went on passionately. "I believe that the very class who was standing the firmest, whose fingers grasp most tightly the sword of warfare, will be most grateful to the people who will wrest the initiative from them and show them the way to an honourable, inevitable peace."

"When do you propose to break those seals?" he enquired.

"To-morrow evening," she replied. "There will be a full meeting of the Council. The terms will be read. Then you shall decide."

E. PHILLIPS OPPENHEIM

"What am I to decide?"

"Whether you will accept the post of spokesman—whether you will be the ambassador who shall approach the Government."

"But they may not elect me," he objected.

"They will," she replied confidently. "It was you who showed them their power. It is you whose inspiration has carried them along: It is you who shall be their representative. Don't you realise," she went on, "that it is the very association of such men as yourself and Miles Furley and the Bishop with this movement which will endow it with reality in the eyes of the bourgeoisie of the country and Parliament?"

Their host returned, followed by his butler carrying a tray with refreshments, and the burden of serious things fell away from them. It was only after Catherine had departed, and the two men lingered for a moment near the fire before retiring, that either of them reverted to the great subject which dominated their thoughts.

"You understand, Julian," the Bishop said, with a shade of anxiety in his tone, "that I am in the same position as yourself so far as regards the proposals which may lie within that envelope? I have joined this movement—or conspiracy, as I suppose it would be called—on the one condition that the terms pronounced there are such as a Christian and a law-loving country, whose children have already made great sacrifices in the cause of freedom, may honourably accept. If they are otherwise, all the weight and influence I may have with the people go into the other scale. I take it that it is so with you?"

"Entirely," Julian acquiesced. "To be frank with you," he added, "my doubts are not so much concerning the terms of peace themselves as the power of the German democracy to enforce them."

"We have relied a good deal," the Bishop admitted, "upon reports from neutrals."

Julian smiled a little grimly.

"We have wasted a good many epithets criticising German diplomacy," he observed, "but she seems to know how to hold most of the neutrals in the hollow of her hand. You know what that Frenchman said? 'Scratch a neutral and you find a German propaganda agent!'"

The Bishop led the way upstairs. Outside the door of Julian's room, he laid his hand affectionately upon the young man's shoulder.

"My godson," he said, "as yet we have scarcely spoken of this great surprise which you have given us—of Paul Fiske. All that I shall say now is this. I am very proud to know that he is my guest to-night.

I am very happy to think that from tomorrow we shall be fellow workers."

CATHERINE, WHILE SHE WAITED FOR her tea in the Carlton lounge on the following afternoon, gazed through the drooping palms which sheltered the somewhat secluded table at which she was seated upon a very brilliant scene. It was just five o'clock, and a packed crowd of fashionable Londoners was listening to the strains of a popular band, or as much of it as could be heard above the din of conversation.

"This is all rather amazing, is it not?" she remarked to her companion.

The latter, an attache at a neutral Embassy, dropped his eyeglass and polished it with a silk handkerchief, in the corner of which was embroidered a somewhat conspicuous coronet.

"It makes an interesting study," he declared. "Berlin now is madly gay, Paris decorous and sober. It remains with London to be normal,— London because its hide is the thickest, its sensibility the least acute, its selfishness the most profound."

Catherine reflected for a moment.

"I think," she said, "that a philosophical history of the war will some day, for those who come after us, be extraordinarily interesting. I mean the study of the national temperaments as they were before, as they are now during the war, and as they will be afterwards. There is one thing which will always be noted, and that is the intense dislike which you, perhaps I, certainly the majority of neutrals, feel towards England."

"It is true," the young man assented solemnly. "One finds it everywhere."

"Before the war," Catherine went on, "it was Germany who was hated everywhere. She pushed her way into the best places at hotels, watering places—Monte Carlo, for instance and the famous spas. Today, all that accumulated dislike seems to be turned upon England. I am not myself a great admirer of this country, and yet I ask myself why?"

"England is smug," the young man pronounced; "She is callous; she is, without meaning to be, hypocritical. She works herself into a terrible state of indignation about the misdeeds of her neighbours, and she does not realise her own faults. The Germans are overbearing, but one realises that and expects it. Englishmen are irritating. It is certainly true that amongst us remaining neutrals," he added, dropping his voice a little and looking around to be sure of their isolation, "the sympathy remains with the Central Powers."

"I have some dear friends in this country, too," Catherine sighed.

"Naturally—amongst those of your own order. But then there is very little difference between the aristocracies of every race in the world. It is the bourgeoisie which tells, which sets its stamp upon a nation's character."

Their tea had arrived, and for a few moments the conversation travelled in lighter channels. The young man, who was a person of some consequence in his own country, spoke easily of the theatres, of mutual friends, of some sport in which he had been engaged. Catherine relapsed into the role which had been her first in life,—the young woman of fashion. As such they attracted no attention save a few admiring glances on the part of passers-by towards Catherine. As the people around them thinned out a little, their conversation became more intimate.

"I shall always feel," the young man said thoughtfully, "that in these days I have lived very near great things. I have seen and realised what the historians will relate at second-hand. The greatest events move like straws in the wind. A month ago, it seemed as though the Central Powers would lose the war."

"I suppose," she observed, "it depends very much upon what you mean by winning it? The terms of peace are scarcely the terms of victory, are they?"

"The terms of peace," he repeated thoughtfully.

"We happen to know what they are, do we not?" she continued, speaking almost under her breath, "the basic terms, at any rate."

"You mean," he said slowly, "the terms put forward by the Socialist Party of Germany to ensure the granting of an armistice?"

"And acceded to," she reminded him, "by the Kaiser and the two greatest German statesmen."

He toyed with his teacup, drew a gold cigarette case from his pocket, selected a cigarette, and lit it.

"You would try to make me believe," he remarked, smiling at his companion, "that to-day you are not in your most intelligent mood."

"Explain, if you please," she begged earnestly.

He smoked stolidly for several moments.

"I imagine," he said, "that you preserve with me something of that very skilfully assumed ignorance which is the true mask of the diplomatist. But is it worth while, I wonder?"

She caught at her breath.

"You are too clever," she murmured, looking at him covertly.

"You have seen," he continued, "how Germany, who needs peace sorely, has striven to use the most despised power in her country for her own advantage—I mean the Socialist Party. From being treated with scorn and ignominy, they were suddenly, at the time of the proposed Stockholm Conference, judged worthy of notice from the All Highest himself. He suddenly saw how wonderful a use might be made of them. It was a very clever trap which was baited, and it was not owing to any foresight or any cleverness on the part of this country that the Allies did not walk straight into it. I say again," he went on, "that it was a mere fluke which prevented the Allies from being represented at that Conference and the driving in of the thin end of the wedge."

"You are quite right," Catherine agreed.

"German diplomacy," he proceeded, "may sometimes be obtuse, but it is at least persistent. Their next move will certainly rank in history as the most astute, the most cunning of any put forward since the war commenced. Of course," the young man went on, fitting his cigarette into a long, amber holder, "we who are not Germans can only guess, but even the guessing is fascinating."

"Go on, please, dear Baron," she begged. "It is when you talk like this and show me your mind that I seem to be listening to a second Bismarck."

"You flatter me, Countess," the young man said, "but indeed these events are interesting. Trace their course for yourself after the failure of Stockholm. The Kaiser has established certain relations with the Socialist Party. Once more he turns towards them. He affects a war weariness he does not feel. He puts it into their heads that they shall approach without molestation certain men in England who have a great Labour following. The plot is started. You know quite well how it has progressed."

"Naturally," Catherine assented, "but after all, tell me, where does the wonderful diplomacy come in? The terms of peace are not the terms of a conqueror. Germany is to engage herself to give up what she has sworn to hold, even to pay indemnities, to restore all conquered countries, and to retire her armies behind the Rhine."

The young man looked at his companion steadfastly for several seconds.

"In the idiom of this country, Countess," he said, "I raise my hat to you. You preserve your mask of ignorance to the end. So much so, indeed, that I find myself asking do you really believe that Germany intends to do this?"

"But you forget," she reminded him. "I was one of those present at the discussion of the preliminaries. The confirmation of the agreed terms, with the signatures, has arrived, and is to be placed before the Labour Council at six o'clock this evening."

The young man for a moment seemed puzzled. Then he glanced at a little gold watch upon his wrist, knocked the cigarette from its holder and carefully replaced the latter in its case.

"That is very interesting, Countess," he said. "For the moment I had forgotten your official position amongst the English Socialists."

She leaned forward and touched his coat sleeve.

"You had forgotten nothing," she declared eagerly. "There is something in your mind of which you have not spoken."

"No," he replied, "I have spoken a great deal of my mind—too much, perhaps, considering that we are seated in this very fashionable lounge, with many people around us. We must talk of these serious matters on another occasion, Countess. I shall pay my respects to your aunt, if I may, within the next few days."

"Why do you fence with me?" she persisted, drawing on her gloves. "You and I both know, so far as regards those peace terms, that—"

"If we both know," he interrupted, "let us keep each our own knowledge. Words are sometimes very dangerous, and great events are looming. So, Countess! You have perhaps a car, or may I have the pleasure of escorting you to your destination?"

"I am going to Westminster," she told him, rising to her feet.

"In that case," he observed, as they made their way down the room, "perhaps I had better not offer my escort, although I should very much like to be there in person. You are amongst those to-day who will make history."

"Come and see me soon," she begged, dropping her voice a little, "and I will confide in you as much as I dare."

"It is tempting," he admitted, "I should like to know what passes at that meeting."

"You can, if you will, dine with us to-morrow night," she invited, "at half-past eight. My aunt will be delighted to see you. I forget whether we have people coming or not, but you will be very welcome."

The young man bowed low as he handed his charge into a taxicab.

"Dear Countess," he murmured, "I shall be charmed."

XV

F or a gathering of men upon whose decision hung such momentous issues, the Council which met that evening at Westminster seemed alike unambitious in tone and uninspired in appearance. Some short time was spent in one of the anterooms, where Julian was introduced to many of the delegates. The disclosure of his identity, although it aroused immense interest, was scarcely an unmixed joy to the majority of them. Those who were in earnest—and they mostly were in grim and deadly earnest—had hoped to find him a man nearer their own class. Fenn and Bright had their own reasons for standing apart, and the extreme pacifists took note of the fact that he had been a soldier. His coming, however, was an event the importance of which nobody attempted to conceal.

The Bishop was voted into the chair when the little company trooped into the apartment which had been set aside for their more important meetings. His election had been proposed by Miles Furley, and as it was announced that under no circumstances would he become a candidate for the permanent leadership of the party, was agreed to without comment. A few notes for his guidance had been jotted down earlier in the day. The great subject of discussion was, of course, the recently received communication from an affiliated body of their friends in Germany, copies of which had been distributed amongst the members.

"I am asked to explain," the Bishop announced, in opening the proceedings, "that this document which we all recognise as being of surpassing importance, has been copied by Mr. Fenn, himself, and that since, copies have been distributed amongst the members, the front door of the building has been closed and the telephones placed under surveillance. It is not, of course, possible that any of you could be mistrusted, but it is of the highest importance that neither the Press, the Government, nor the people should have any indication of what is transpiring, until the delegate whom you choose takes the initial step. It is proposed that until after his interview with the Prime Minister, no delegate shall leave the place. The question now arises, what of the terms themselves? I will ask each one of you to state his views, commencing with Miss Abbeway."

Every one of the twenty-three—or twenty-four now, including Julian—had a few words to say, and the tenor of their remarks was identical. For a basis of peace terms, the proposals were entirely reasonable, nor did they appear in any case to be capable of misconstruction. They were laid down in eight clauses.

1. The complete evacuation of Northern France and Belgium, with full compensation for all damage done.
2. Alsace and Lorraine to determine their position by vote of the entire population.
3. Servia and Roumania to be reestablished as independent kingdoms, with such rectifications and modifications of frontier as a joint committee should decide upon.
4. The German colonies to be restored.
5. The conquered parts of Mesopotamia to remain under the protection of the British Government.
6. Poland to be declared an independent kingdom.
7. Trieste and certain portions of the Adriatic seaboard to be ceded to Italy.
8. A world committee to be at once elected for the purpose of working out a scheme of international disarmament.

"We must remember," Miles Furley pointed out, "that the present Government is practically pledged not to enter into peace negotiations with a Hohenzollern."

"That, I contend," the Bishop observed, "is a declaration which should never have been made. Whatever may be our own feelings with regard to the government of Germany, the Kaiser has held the nation together and is at the present moment its responsible head. If he has had the good sense to yield to the demands of his people, as is proved by this document, then it is very certain that the declaration must be forgotten. I have reason to believe, however, that even if the negotiations have been commenced in the name of the Kaiser, an immediate change is likely to take place in the constitution of Germany."

"Germany's new form of government, I understand," Fenn intervened, "will be modelled upon our own, which, after the abolition of the House of Lords, and the abnegation of the King's prerogative, will be as near the ideal democracy as is possible. That change will be in itself our most potent guarantee against all future wars. No democracy ever encouraged bloodshed. It is, to my mind, a clearly proved fact that all wars are the result of court intrigue. There will be no more of that. The passing of monarchical rule in Germany will mean the doom of all autocracies."

There was a little sympathetic murmur. Julian, to whom Catherine had been whispering, next asked a question.

"I suppose," he said, "that no doubt can be cast upon the authenticity of the three signatures attached to this document?"

"That's been in my own mind, Mr. Fiske—leastwise, Mr. Orden," Phineas Cross, the Northumbrian, remarked, from the other side of the table. "They're up to any mortal dodge, these Germans. Are we to accept it as beyond all doubt that this document is entirely genuine?"

"How can we do otherwise?" Fenn demanded. "Freistner, who is responsible for it, has been in unofficial correspondence with us since the commencement of the war. We know his handwriting, we know his character, we've had a hundred different occasions to test his earnestness and trustworthiness. This document is in his own writing and accompanied by remarks and references to previous correspondence which render its authenticity indisputable."

"Granted that the proposals themselves are genuine, there still remain the three signatures," Julian observed.

"Why should we doubt them?" Fenn protested. "Freistner guarantees them, and Freistner is our friend, the friend and champion of Labour throughout the world. To attempt to deceive us would be to cover himself with eternal obloquy."

"Yet these terms," Julian pointed out, "differ fundamentally from anything which Germany has yet allowed to be made public."

"There are two factors here which may be considered," Miles Furley intervened. "The first is that the economic condition of Germany is far worse than she has allowed us to know. The second, which is even more interesting to us, is the rapid growth in influence, power, and numbers of the Socialist and Labour Party in that country."

"Of both these factors," the Bishop reminded them, "we have had very frequent hints from our friends, the neutrals. Let me tell you all what I think. I think that those terms are as much as we have the right to expect, even if our armies had reached the Rhine. It is possible that we might obtain some slight modifications, if we continued the war, but would those modifications be worth the loss of a few more hundred thousands of human lives, of a few more months of this hideous, pagan slaughter and defilement of God's beautiful world?"

There was a murmur of approval. A lank, rawboned Yorkshireman— David Sands—a Wesleyan enthusiast, a local preacher, leaned across the table, his voice shaking with earnestness:

"It's true!" he exclaimed. "It's the word of God! It's for us to stop the war. If we stop it to-night instead of to-morrow, a thousand lives may be saved, human lives, lives of our fellow creatures. Our fellow labourers in Germany have given us the chance. Don't let us delay five minutes. Let the one of us you may select see the Prime Minister to-night and deliver the people's message."

"There's no cause for delay that I can see," Cross approved.

"There is none," Fenn assented heartily. "I propose that we proceed to the election of our representative; that, having elected him, we send him to the Prime Minister with our message, and that we remain here in the building until we have his report."

"You are unanimously resolved, then," the Bishop asked, "to take this last step?"

There was a little chorus of assent. Fenn leaned forward in his place.

"Everything is ready," he announced. "Our machinery is perfect. Our agents in every city await the mandate."

"But do you imagine that those last means will be necessary?" the Bishop enquired anxiously.

"Most surely I do," Fenn replied. "Remember that if the people make peace for the country, it is the people who will expect to govern the country. It will be a notice to the politicians to quit. They know that. It is my belief that they will resist, tooth and nail."

Bright glanced at his watch.

"The Prime Minister," he announced, "will be at Downing Street until nine o'clock. It is now seven o'clock. I propose that we proceed without any further delay to the election of our representative."

"The voting cards," Fenn pointed out, "are before each person. Every one has two votes, which must be for two different representatives. The cards should then be folded, and I propose that the Bishop, who is not a candidate, collect them. As I read the unwritten rules of this Congress, every one here is eligible except the Bishop, Miss Abbeway, Mr. Orden and Mr. Furley."

There was a little murmur. Phineas Cross leaned forward in his place.

"Here, what's that?" he exclaimed. "The Bishop, and Miss Abbeway, we all know, are outside the running. Mr. Furley, too, represents the educated Socialists, and though he is with us in this, he is not really Labour. But Mr. Orden—Paul Fiske, eh? That's a different matter, isn't it?"

"Mr. Orden," Fenn pronounced slowly, "is a literary man. He is a sympathiser with our cause, but he is not of it."

"If any man has read the message which Paul Fiske has written with a pen of gold for us," Phineas Cross declared, "and can still say that he is not one of us, why, he must be beside himself. I say that Mr. Orden is the brains and the soul of our movement. He brought life and encouragement into the north of England with the first article he ever wrote. Since then there has not been a man whom the Labour Party that I know anything of has looked up to and worshipped as they have done him."

"It's true," David Sands broke in, "every word of it. There's no one has written for Labour like him. If he isn't Labour, then we none of us are. I don't care whether he is the son of an earl, or a plasterer's apprentice, as I was. He's the right stuff, he has the gift of putting the words together, and his heart's where it should be."

"There is no one," Fenn said, his voice trembling a little, "who has a greater admiration for Paul Fiske's writings than I have, but I still contend that he is not Labour."

"Sit down, lad," Cross enjoined. "We'll have a vote on that. I'm for saying that Mr. Julian Orden here, who has written them articles under the name of 'Paul Fiske', is a full member of our Council and eligible to act as our messenger to the Prime Minister. I ask the Bishop to put it to the meeting."

Eighteen were unanimous in agreeing with the motion. Fenn sat down, speechless. His cheeks were pallid. His hands, which rested upon the table, were twitching. He seemed like a man lost in thought and only remembered to fill up his card when the Bishop asked him for it. There was a brief silence whilst the latter, assisted by Cross and Sands, counted the votes. Then the Bishop rose to his feet.

"Mr. Julian Orden," he announced, "better known to you all under the name of 'Paul Fiske', has been chosen by a large majority as your representative to take the people's message to the Prime Minister."

"I protest!" Fenn exclaimed passionately. "This is Mr. Orden's first visit amongst us. He is a stranger. I repeat that he is not one of us. Where is his power? He has none. Can he do what any one of us can— stop the pulse of the nation? Can he still its furnace fires? Can he empty the shipyards and factories, hold the trains upon their lines, bring the miners up from under the earth? Can he—"

"He can do all these things," Phineas Cross interrupted, "because he speaks for us, our duly elected representative. Sit thee down, Fenn. If you wanted the job, well, you haven't got it, and that's all there is about it, and though you're as glib with your tongue as any here, and though you've as many at your back, perchance, as I have, I tell you I'd never have voted for you if there hadn't been another man here. So put that in your pipe and smoke it, lad."

"All further discussion," the Bishop ruled, "is out of order. Julian Orden, do you accept this mission?"

Julian rose to his feet. He leaned heavily upon his stick. His expression was strangely disturbed.

"Bishop," he said, "and you, my friends, this has all come very suddenly. I do not agree with Mr. Fenn. I consider that I am one with you. I think that for the last ten years I have seen the place which Labour should hold in the political conduct of the world. I have seen the danger of letting the voice of the people remain unheard too long. Russia to-day is a practical and terrible example of that danger. England is, in her way, a free country, and our Government a good one, but in the world's history there arrive sometimes crises with which no stereotyped form of government can cope, when the one thing that is desired is the plain, honest mandate of those who count for most in the world, those who, in their simplicity and in their absence from all political ties and precedents and liaisons, see the truth. That is why I have appealed with my pen to Labour, to end this war. That is why I shall go willingly as your representative to the Prime Minister to-night."

The Bishop held out his hand. There was a little reverent hush, for his words were in the nature of a benediction.

"And may God be with you, our messenger," he said solemnly.

XVI

Julian, duly embarked upon his mission, was kept waiting an unexpectedly short time in the large but gloomy apartment into which Mr. Stenson's butler had somewhat doubtfully ushered him. The Prime Minister entered with an air of slight hurry. He was also somewhat surprised.

"My dear Orden," he exclaimed, holding out his hand, "what can I do for you?"

"A great deal," Julian replied gravely. "First of all, though, I have an explanation to make."

"I am afraid," Mr. Stenson regretted, "that I am too much engaged this evening to enter into any personal matters. I am expecting a messenger here on very important official business."

"I am that messenger," Julian announced.

Mr. Stenson started. His visitor's tone was serious and convincing.

"I fear that we are at loggerheads. It is an envoy from the Labour Party whom I am expecting."

"I am that envoy."

"You?" Mr. Stenson exclaimed, in blank bewilderment.

"I ought to explain a little further, perhaps. I have been writing on Labour questions for some time under the pseudonym of 'Paul Fiske'."

"Paul Fiske?" Mr. Stenson gasped. "You—Paul Fiske?"

Julian nodded assent.

"You are amazed, of course," he proceeded, "but it is nevertheless the truth. The fact has just come to light, and I have been invited to join this new emergency Council, composed of one or two Socialists and writers, amongst them a very distinguished prelate; Labour Members of Parliament, and representatives of the various Trades Unions, a body of men which you doubtless know all about. I attended a meeting at Westminster an hour ago, and I was entrusted with this commission to you."

Mr. Stenson sat down suddenly.

"God bless my soul!" he exclaimed. "You—Julian Orden!"

There was a moment's silence. Mr. Stenson, however, was a man of immense recuperative powers. He assimilated the new situation without further protest.

"You have given me the surprise of my life, Orden," he confessed.

"That, however, is a personal matter. Hannaway Wells is in the study. You have no objection, I suppose, to his being present?"

"None whatever."

Mr. Stenson rang the bell, and in a few minutes they were joined by his colleague. The former wasted no time in explanations.

"You will doubtless be as astonished as I was, Wells," he said, "to learn that our friend Julian Orden comes here as the representative of the new Labour Council. His qualifications, amongst others, are that under the pseudonym of 'Paul Fiske' he is the writer of those wonderful articles which have been the beacon light and the inspiration of the Labour Party for the last year."

Mr. Hannaway Wells prided himself upon never being surprised. This time the only way he could preserve his reputation was by holding his tongue.

"We are now prepared to hear your mission," Mr. Stenson continued, turning to his visitor.

"I imagine," Julian began, "that you know something about this new Labour Council?"

"What little we do know," Mr. Stenson answered, "we have learnt with great difficulty through our secret service. I gather that a small league of men has been formed within a mile of the Houses of Parliament, who, whatever their motives may be, have been guilty of treasonable and traitorous communication with the enemy."

"Strictly speaking, you are, without doubt, perfectly right," Julian acknowledged.

Mr. Stenson switched on an electric light.

"Sit down, Orden," he invited. "There is no need for us to stand glaring at one another. There is enough of real importance in the nature of our interview without making melodrama of it."

The Prime Minister threw himself into an easy chair. Julian, with a little sigh of relief, selected a high-backed oak chair and rested his foot upon a hassock. Hannaway Wells remained standing upon the hearthrug.

"Straight into the heart of it, please, Orden," Mr. Stenson begged. "Let us know how far this accursed conspiracy has gone."

"It has gone to very great lengths," Julian declared. "Certain members of this newly-formed Council of Labour have been in communication for some months with the Socialist Party in Germany. From these latter they have received a definite and authentic proposal of peace, countersigned by the three most important men in Germany. That proposal of peace I am here to lay before you, with the request that you act upon it without delay."

Julian produced his roll of papers. The two men remained motionless. The great issue had been reached with almost paralysing rapidity.

"My advice," Mr. Hannaway Wells said bluntly, "is that you, sir,"—turning to his Chief—"refuse to discuss or consider these proposals, or to examine that document. I submit that you are the head of His Majesty's Government, and any communication emanating from a foreign country should be addressed to you. If you ever consider this matter and discuss it with Mr. Orden here, you associate yourself with a traitorous breach of the law."

Mr. Stenson made no immediate reply. He looked towards Julian, as though to hear what he had to say.

"Mr. Hannaway Wells's advice is, without doubt, technically correct," Julian admitted, "but the whole subject is too great, and the issues involved too awful for etiquette or even propriety to count. It is for you, sir, to decide what is best for the country. You commit yourself to nothing by reading the proposals, and I suggest that you do so."

"We will read them," Mr. Stenson decided.

Julian passed over the papers. The two men crossed the room and leaned over the Prime Minister's writing table. Mr. Stenson drew down the electric light, and they remained there in close confabulation for about a quarter of an hour. Julian sat with his back turned towards them and his ears closed. In this atmosphere of government, his own position seemed to him weird and fantastic. A sense of unreality cumbered his thoughts. Even this brief pause in the actual negotiations filled him with doubts. He could scarcely believe that it was he who was to dictate terms to the man who was responsible for the government of the country; that it was he who was to force a decision pregnant with far-reaching consequences to the entire world. The figures of Fenn and Bright loomed up ominously before him, however hard he tried to push them into the background. Was it the mandate of such men as these that he was carrying?

Presently the two Ministers returned to their places. Julian had heard their voices for the last few minutes without being able to distinguish a word of their actual conversation.

"We have considered the document you have brought, Orden," the Prime Minister said, "and we frankly admit that we find its contents surprising. The terms of peace suggested form a perfectly possible basis for negotiations. At the same time, you are probably aware that it has not been in the mind of His Majesty's Ministers to discuss terms of peace at all with the present administration of Germany."

"These terms," Julian reminded him, "are dictated, not by the Kaiser and his advisers, but by the Socialist and Labour Party."

"It is strange," Mr. Stenson pointed out, "that we have heard so little of that Party. It is even astonishing that we should find them in a position to be able to dictate terms of peace to the Hohenzollerns."

"You do not dispute the authenticity of the document?" Julian asked.

"I will not go so far as that," Mr. Stenson replied cautiously. "Our secret service informed us some time ago that Freistner, the head of the German Socialists, was in communication with certain people in this country. I have no doubt whatever that these are the proposals of the authorised Socialist Party of Germany. What I do not understand is how they have suddenly acquired the strength to induce proposals of peace such as these."

"It has been suggested," Julian said, "that even the Hohenzollerns, even the military clique of Germany, see before them now the impossibility of reaping the rewards of their successful campaigns. Peace is becoming a necessity to them. They would prefer, therefore, to seem to yield to the demands of their own Socialists rather than to foreign pressure."

"That may be so," Mr. Stenson admitted. "Let us proceed. The first part of your duty, Orden, is finished. What else have you to say?"

"I am instructed," Julian announced, "to appeal to you to sue at once, through the Spanish Ambassador, for an armistice while these terms are considered and arrangements made for discussing them."

"And if I refuse?"

"I will not evade even that question. Of the twenty-three members of the new Council of Labour, twenty represent the Trades Unions of the great industries of the kingdom. Those twenty will unanimously proclaim a general strike, if you should refuse the proposed armistice."

"In other words," Mr. Stenson observed drily, "they will scuttle the ship themselves. Do you approve of these tactics?"

"I decline to answer that question," Julian said, "but I would point out to you that when you acknowledged yourself defeated by the miners of South Wales, you pointed the way to some such crisis as this."

"That may be true," Mr. Stenson acknowledged. "I have only at this moment, however, to deal with the present condition of affairs. Do you seriously believe that, if I make the only answer which at present seems to me possible, the Council of Labour, as they call themselves, will adopt the measures they threaten?"

"I believe that they will," Julian declared gravely. "I believe that the country looks upon any continuation of this war as a continuation of unnecessary and ghastly slaughter. To appreciably change the military situation would mean the sacrifice of millions more lives, would mean the continuation of the war for another two years. I believe that the people of Germany who count are of the same opinion. I believe that the inevitable change of government in Germany will show us a nation freed from this hideous lust for conquest, a nation with whom, when she is purged of the poison of these last years, we can exist fraternally and with mutual benefit."

"You are a very sanguine man, Mr. Orden," Hannaway Wells remarked.

"I have never found," Julian replied, "that the pessimist walks with his head turned towards the truth."

"How long have I," the Prime Minister asked, after a brief pause, "for my reply?"

"Twenty-four hours," Julian told him, "during which time it is hoped that you will communicate with our Allies and pave the way for a further understanding. The Council of Labour asks you for no pledge as to their safety. We know quite well that all of us are, legally speaking, guilty of treason. On the other hand, a single step towards the curtailment of our liberties will mean the paralysis of every industry in the United Kingdom."

"I realise the position perfectly," Mr. Stenson observed drily. "I do not exactly know what to say to you personally, Orden," he added. "Perhaps it is as well for us that the Council should have chosen an ambassador with whom discussion, at any rate, is possible. Nevertheless, I feel bound to remind you that you have taken upon your shoulders, considering your birth and education, one of the most perilous loads which any man could carry."

"I have weighed the consequences," Julian replied, with a sudden and curious sadness in his tone. "I know how the name of 'pacifist' stinks in the nostrils. I know how far we are committed as a nation to a peace won by force of arms. I know how our British blood boils at the thought of leaving a foreign country with as many military advantages as Germany has acquired. But I feel, too, that there is the other side.

I have brought you evidence that it is not the German nation against whom we fight, man against man, human being against human being. It is my belief that autocracy and the dynasty of the Hohenzollerns will crumble into ruin as a result of today's negotiations, just as surely as though we sacrificed God knows how many more lives to achieve a greater measure of military triumph."

The Prime Minister rang the bell.

"You are an honest man, Julian Orden," he said, "and a decent emissary. You will reply that we take the twenty-four hours for reflection. That means that we shall meet at nine o'clock to-morrow evening."

He held out his hand in farewell, an action which somehow sent Julian away a happier man.

XVII

Julian, on, the morning following his visit to the Prime Minister, was afflicted with a curious and persistent unrest. He travelled down to the Temple land found Miles Furley in a room hung with tobacco smoke and redolent of a late night.

"Miles," Julian declared, as the two men shook hands, "I can't rest."

"I am in the same fix," Furley admitted. "I sat here till four o'clock. Phineas Cross came around, and half-a-dozen of the others. I felt I must talk to them, I must keep on hammering it out. We're right, Julian. We must be right!"

"It's a ghastly responsibility. I wonder what history will have to say."

"That's the worst of it," Furley groaned. "They'll have a bird's-eye view of the whole affair, those people who write our requiem or our eulogy. You noticed the Press this morning? They're all hinting at some great move in the West. It's about in the clubs. Why, I even heard last night that we were in Ostend. It's all a rig, of course. Stenson wants to gain time."

"Who opened these negotiations with Freistner?" Julian asked.

"Fenn. He met him at the Geneva Conference, the year before the war. I met him, too, but I didn't see so much of him. He's a fine fellow, Julian—as unlike the typical German as any man you ever met."

"He's honest, I suppose?"

"As the day itself," was the confident reply. "He has been in prison twice, you know, for plain speaking. He is the one man in Germany who has fought the war, tooth and nail, from the start."

Julian caught his friend by the shoulder.

"Miles," he said,—"straight from the bottom of your heart, mind— you do believe we are justified?"

"I have never doubted it."

"You know that we have practically created a revolution—that we have established a dictatorship? Stenson must obey or face anarchy."

"It is the voice of the people," Furley declared. "I am convinced that we are justified. I am convinced of the inutility of the prolongation of this war."

Julian drew a little sigh of relief.

"Don't think I am weakening," he said. "Remember, I am new to this thing in practice, even though I may be responsible for some of the theory."

"It is the people who are the soundest directors of a nation's policy," Furley pronounced. "High politics becomes too much like a game of chess, hedged all around with etiquette and precedent. It's human life we want to save, Julian. People don't stop to realise the horrible tragedy of even one man's death—one man with his little circle of relatives and friends. In the game of war one forgets. Human beings—men from the toiler's bench, the carpenter's bench, from behind the counter, from the land, from the mine—don khaki, become soldiers, and there seems something different about them. So many human lives gone every day; just soldiers, just the toll we have to pay for a slight advance or a costly retreat. And, my God, every one of them, underneath their khaki, is a human being! The politicians don't grasp it, Julian. That's our justification. The day that armistice is signed, several hundred lives at least—perhaps, thousands—will be saved; for several hundred women the sun will continue to shine. Parents, sweethearts, children—all of them—think what they will be spared!"

"I am a man again," Julian declared. "Come along round to Westminster. There are many things I want to ask about the Executive."

They drove round to the great building which had been taken over by the different members of the Labour Council. The representative of each Trades Union had his own office, staff of clerks and private telephone. Fenn, who greeted the two men with a rather excessive cordiality, constituted himself their cicerone. He took them from room to room and waited while Julian exchanged remarks with some of the delegates whom he had not met personally.

"Every one of our members," Fenn pointed out, "is in direct communication with the local secretary of each town in which his industry is represented. You see these?"

He paused and laid his hand on a little heap of telegraph forms, on which one word was typed.

"These," he continued, "are all ready to be dispatched the second that we hear from Mr. Stenson that is to say if we should hear unfavourably. They are divided into batches, and each batch will be sent from a different post-office, so that there shall be no delay. We calculate that in seven hours, at the most, the industrial pulse of the country will have ceased to beat."

"How long has your organisation taken to build up?" Julian enquired.

"Exactly three months," David Sands observed, turning around in his swing chair from the desk at which he had been writing. "The scheme was started a few days after your article in the British Review. We took your motto as our text 'Coordination and cooperation.'"

They found their way into the clubroom, and at luncheon, later on, Julian strove to improve his acquaintance with the men who were seated around him. Some of them were Members of Parliament with well-known names, others were intensely local, but all seemed earnest and clear-sighted. Phineas Cross commenced to talk about war generally. He had just returned from a visit with other Labour Members to the front, although it is doubtful whether the result had been exactly in accordance with the intentions of the powers who had invited him.

"I'll tell you something about war," he said, "which contradicts most every other experience. There's scarcely a great subject in the world which you don't have to take as a whole, and from the biggest point of view, to appreciate it thoroughly. It's exactly different with war. If you want to understand more than the platitudes, you want to just take in one section of the fighting. Say there are fifty Englishmen, decent fellows, been dragged from their posts as commercial travellers or small tradesmen or labourers or what-not, and they get mixed up with a similar number of Germans. Those Germans ain't the fiends we read about. They're not bubbling over with militarism. They don't want to lord it over all the world. They've exactly the same tastes, the same outlook upon life as the fifty Englishmen whom an iron hand has been forcing to do their best to kill. Those English chaps didn't want to kill anybody, any more than the Germans did. They had to do it, too, simply because it was part of the game. There was a handful of German prisoners I saw, talking with their guard and exchanging smokes. One was a barber in a country town. The man who had him in tow was an English barber. Bless you, they were talking like one o'clock! That German barber didn't want anything in life except plenty to eat and drink, to be a good husband and good father, and to save enough money to buy a little house of his own. The Englishman was just the same. He'd as soon have had that German for a pal for a day's fishing or a walk in the country, as any one else. They'd neither of them got anything against the other. Where the hell is this spirit of hatred? You go down the line, mile after mile, and most little groups of men facing one another are just the same. Here and there, there's some bitter feeling, through some fighting that's seemed unfair, but that's nothing. The fact remains that those millions of men don't hate one another, that they've got nothing to hate one another about, and they're being driven to slaughter one another like savage beasts. For what? Mr. Stenson might supply an answer. Your great editors might. Your great Generals could be glib about it. They could spout volumes of words, but there's no substance about them. I say that in this generation there's no call for fighting, and there didn't ought to be any."

"You are not only right, but you are splendidly right, Mr. Cross," Julian declared. "It's human talk, that."

"It's just a plain man's words and thoughts," was the simple reply.

"And yet," Fenn complained, in his thin voice, "if I talk like that, they call me a pacifist, a lot of rowdies get up and sing 'Rule Britannia', and try to chivy me out of the hall where I'm speaking."

"You see, there's a difference, lad," Cross pointed out, setting down the tankard of beer from which he had been drinking. "You talk sometimes that white-livered stuff about not hitting a man back if he wants to hit you, and you drag in your conscience, and prate about all men being brothers, and that sort of twaddle. A full-blooded Englishman don't like it, because we are all of us out to protect what we've got, any way and anyhow. But that doesn't alter the fact that there's something wrong in the world when we're driven to do this protecting business wholesale and being forced into murdering on a scale which only devils could have thought out and imagined. It's the men at the top that are responsible for this war, and when people come to reckon up, they'll say that there was blame up at the top in the Government of every Power that's fighting, but there was a damned sight more blame amongst the Germans than any of the others, and that's why many a hundred thousand of our young men who've loathed the war and felt about it as I do have gone and done their bit and kept their mouths shut."

"You cannot deny," Fenn argued, "that war is contrary to Christianity."

"I dunno, lad," Cross replied, winking across the table at Julian. "Seems to me there was a powerful lot of fighting in the Old Testament, and the Lord was generally on one side or the other. But you and I ain't going to bicker, Mr. Fenn. The first decision this Council came to, when it embraced more than a dozen of us of very opposite ways of thinking, was to keep our mouths shut about our own ideas and stick to business. So give me a fill of baccy from your pipe, and we'll have a cup of coffee together."

Julian's pouch was first upon the table, and the Northumbrian filled his pipe in leisurely fashion.

"Good stuff, sir," he declared approvingly, as he passed it back. "After dinner I am mostly a man of peace—even when Fenn comes yapping around," he added, looking after the disappearing figure of the secretary. "But I make no secret of this. I tumbled to it from the first that this was a great proposition, this amalgamation of Labour. It makes a power of us, even though it may, as you, Mr. Orden, said in one of your articles, bring us to the gates of revolution. But it was all I could do to bring myself to sit down at the same table with Fenn and his friend Bright. You see," he explained, "there may be times when you are forced into doing a thing that fundamentally you disapprove of and you know is wrong. I disapprove of this war, and I know it's wrong—it's a foul mess that we've been got into by those who should have known better—but I ain't like Fenn about it. We're in it, and we've got to get out of it, not like cowards but like Englishmen, and if fighting had been the only way through, then I should have been for fighting to the last gasp. Fortunately, we've got into touch with the sensible folk on the other side. If we hadn't—well, I'll say no more but that I've got two boys fighting and one buried at Ypres, and I've another, though he's over young, doing his drill."

"Mr. Cross," Julian said, "you've done me more good than any one I've talked to since the war began."

"That's right, lad," Cross replied. "You get straight words from one; and not only that, you get the words of another million behind me, who feel as I do. But," he added, glancing across the room and lowering his voice, "keep your eye on that artful devil, Fenn. He doesn't bear you any particular good will."

"He wasn't exactly a hospitable gaoler," Julian reminiscently observed.

"I'm not speaking of that only," Cross went on. "There wasn't one of us who didn't vote for squeezing that document out of you one way or the other, and if it had been necessary to screw your neck off for it, I don't know as one of us would have hesitated, for you were standing between us and the big thing. But he and that little skunk Bright ain't to be trusted, in my mind, and it seems to me they've got a down on you. Fenn counted on being heart of this Council, for one thing, and there's a matter of a young woman, eh, for another?"

"A young woman?" Julian repeated.

Cross nodded.

"The Russian young person—Miss Abbeway, she calls herself. Fenn's been her lap-dog round here—takes her out to dine and that. It's just a word of warning, that's all. You're new amongst us, Mr. Orden, and you might think us all honest men. Well, we ain't; that's all there is to it."

Julian recovered from a momentary fit of astonishment.

"I am much obliged to you for your candour, Mr. Cross," he said.

"And never you mind about the 'Mr.', sir," the Northumbrian begged.

"Nor you about the 'sir'," Julian retorted, with a smile.

"Middle stump," Cross acknowledged. "And since we are on the subject, my new friend, let me tell you this. To feel perfectly happy about this Council, there's just three as I should like to see out of it— Fenn, Bright—and the young lady."

"Why the young lady?" Julian asked quickly.

"You might as well ask me, 'Why Fenn and Bright?'" the other replied. "I shouldn't make no answer. We're superstitious, you know, we north country folk, and we are all for instincts. All I can say to you is that there isn't one of those three I'd trust around the corner."

"Miss Abbeway is surely above suspicion?" Julian protested. "She has given up a great position and devoted the greater part of her fortune towards the causes which you and I and all of us are working for."

"There'd be plenty of work for her in Russia just now," Cross observed.

"No person of noble birth," Julian reminded him, "has the slightest chance of working effectively in Russia to-day. Besides, Miss Abbeway is half English. Failing Russia, she would naturally select this as the country in which she could do most good."

Some retort seemed to fade away upon the other's lips. His shaggy eyebrows were drawn a little closer together as he glanced towards the door. Julian followed the direction of his gaze. Catherine had entered and was looking around as though in search of some one.

Catherine was more heavily veiled than usual. Her dress and hat were of sombre black, and her manner nervous and disturbed. She came slowly towards their end of the table, although she was obviously in search of some one else.

"Do you happen to know where Mr. Fenn is?" she enquired.

Julian raised his eyebrows.

"Fenn was here a few minutes ago," he replied, "but he left us abruptly. I fancy that he rather disapproved of our conversation."

"He has gone to his room perhaps," she said. "I will go upstairs."

She turned away. Julian, however, followed her to the door.

"Shall I see you again before you leave?" he asked.

"Of course—if you wish to."

There was a moment's perceptible pause.

"Won't you come upstairs with me to Mr. Fenn's room?" she continued.

"Not if your business is in any way private."

She began to ascend the stairs.

"It isn't private," she said, "but I particularly want Mr. Fenn to tell me something, and as you know, he is peculiar. Perhaps, if you don't mind, it would be better if you waited for me downstairs."

Julian's response was a little vague. She left him, however, without appearing to notice his reluctance and knocked at the door of Fenn's room. She found him seated behind a desk, dictating some letters to a stenographer, whom he waved away at her entrance.

"Delighted to see you, Miss Abbeway," he declared impressively, "delighted! Come and sit down, please, and talk to me. We have had a tremendous morning. Even though the machine is all ready to start, it needs a watchful hand all the time."

She sank into the chair from which he had swept a pile of papers and raised her veil.

"Mr. Fenn," she confessed. "I came to you because I have been very worried."

He withdrew a little into himself. His eyes narrowed. His manner became more cautious.

"Worried?" he repeated. "Well?"

"I want to ask you this: have you heard anything from Freistner during the last day or two?"

Fenn's face was immovable. He still showed no signs of discomposure—his voice only was not altogether natural.

"Last day or two?" he repeated reflectively. "No, I can't say that I have, Miss Abbeway. I needn't remind you that we don't risk communications except when they are necessary."

"Will you try and get into touch with him at once?" she begged.

"Why?" Fenn asked, glancing at her searchingly.

"One of our Russian writers," she said, "once wrote that there are a thousand eddies in the winds of chance. One of those has blown my way to-day—or rather yesterday. Freistner is above all suspicion, is he not?"

"Far above," was the confident reply. "I am not the only one who knows him. Ask the others."

"Do you think it possible that he himself can have been deceived?" she persisted.

"In what manner?"

"In his own strength—the strength of his own Party," she proceeded eagerly. "Do you think it possible that the Imperialists have pretended to recognise in him a far greater factor in the situation than he really is? Have pretended to acquiesce in these terms of peace with the intention of repudiating them when we have once gone too far?"

Fenn seemed for a moment to have shrunk in his chair. His eyes had fallen before her passionate gaze. The penholder which he was grasping snapped in his fingers. Nevertheless, his voice still performed its office.

"My dear Miss Abbeway," he protested, "who or what has been putting these ideas into your head?"

"A veritable chance," she replied, "brought me yesterday afternoon into contact with a man—a neutral—who is supposed to be very intimately acquainted with what goes on in Germany."

"What did he tell you?" Fenn demanded feverishly.

"He told me nothing," she admitted. "I have no more to go on than an uplifted eyebrow. All the same, I came away feeling uneasy. I have felt wretched ever since. I am wretched now. I beg you to get at once into touch with Freistner. You can do that now without any risk. Simply ask him for a confirmation of the existing situation."

"That is quite easy," Fenn promised. "I will do it without delay. But in the meantime," he added, moistening his dry lips, "can't you possibly get to know what this man—this neutral—is driving at?"

"I fear not," she replied, "but I shall try. I have invited him to dine to-night."

"If you discover anything, when shall you let us know?"

"Immediately," she promised. "I shall telephone for Mr. Orden."

For a moment he lost control of himself.

"Why Mr. Orden?" he demanded passionately. "He is the youngest member of the Council. He knows nothing of our negotiations with Freistner. Surely I am the person with whom you should communicate?"

"It will be very late to-night," she reminded him, "and Mr. Orden is my personal friend—outside the Council."

"And am I not?" he asked fiercely. "I want to be. I have tried to be."

She appeared to find his agitation disconcerting, and she withdrew a little from the yellow-stained fingers which had crept out towards hers.

"We are all friends," she said evasively. "Perhaps—if there is anything important, then—I will come, or send for you."

He rose to his feet, less, it seemed, as an act of courtesy in view of her departure, than with the intention of some further movement. He suddenly reseated himself, however, his fingers grasped at the air, he became ghastly pale.

"Are you ill, Mr. Fenn?" she exclaimed.

He poured himself out a glass of water with trembling fingers and drank it unsteadily.

"Nerves, I suppose," he said. "I've had to carry the whole burden of these negotiations upon my shoulders, with very little help from any one, with none of the sympathy that counts."

A momentary impulse of kindness did battle with her invincible dislike of the man.

"You must remember," she urged, "that yours is a glorious work; that our thoughts and gratitude are with you."

"But are they?" he demanded, with another little burst of passion. "Gratitude, indeed! If the Council feel that, why was I not selected to approach the Prime Minister instead of Julian Orden? Sympathy! If you, the one person from whom I desire it, have any to offer, why can you not be kinder? Why can you not respond, ever so little, to what I feel for you?"

She hesitated for a moment, seeking for the words which would hurt him least. Tactless as ever, he misunderstood her.

"I may have had one small check in my career," he continued eagerly, "but the game is not finished. Believe me, I have still great cards up my sleeve. I know that you have been used to wealth and luxury. Miss Abbeway," he went on, his voice dropping to a hoarse whisper, "I was not boasting the other night. I have saved money, I have speculated fortunately—I—"

The look in her eyes stifled his eloquence. He broke off in his speech—became dumb and voiceless.

"Mr. Fenn," she said, "once and for all this sort of conversation is distasteful to me. A great deal of what you say I do not understand. What I do understand, I dislike."

She left him, with an inscrutable look. He made no effort to open the door for her. He simply stood listening to her departing footsteps, listened to the shrill summons of the lift-bell, listened to the lift itself go clanging downwards. Then he resumed his seat at his desk. With his hands clasped nervously together, an ink smear upon his cheek, his mouth slightly open, disclosing his irregular and discoloured teeth, he was not by any means a pleasant looking object.

He blew down a tube by his side and gave a muttered order. In a few minutes Bright presented himself.

"I am busy," the latter observed curtly, as he closed the door behind him.

"You've got to be busier in a few minutes," was the harsh reply. "There's a screw loose somewhere."

Bright stood motionless.

"Any one been disagreeable?" he asked, after a moment's pause.

"Get down to your office at once," Fenn directed briefly. "Have Miss Abbeway followed. I want reports of her movements every hour. I shall be here all night."

Bright grinned unpleasantly.

"Another Samson, eh?"

"Go to Hell, and do as you're told!" was the fierce reply. "Put your best men on the job. I must know, for all our sakes, the name of the neutral whom Miss Abbeway sees to-night and with whom she is exchanging confidences."

Bright left the room with a shrug of the shoulders. Nicholas Fenn turned up the electric light, pulled out a bank book from the drawer of his desk, and, throwing it on to the fire, watched it until it was consumed.

XVIII

The Baron Hellman, comfortably seated at the brilliantly decorated round dining table, between Catherine, on one side, and a lady to whom he had not been introduced, contemplated the menu through his immovable eyeglass with satisfaction, unfolded his napkin, and continued the conversation with his hostess, a few places away, which the announcement of dinner had interrupted.

"You are quite right, Princess," he admitted.

"The position of neutrals, especially in the diplomatic world, becomes, in the case of a war like this, most difficult and sometimes embarrassing. To preserve a correct attitude is often a severe strain upon one's self-restraint."

The Princess nodded sympathetically.

"A very charming young man, the Baron," she confided to the General who had taken her in to dinner. "I knew his father and his uncle quite well, in those happy days before the war, when one used to move from country to country."

"Diplomatic type of features," the General remarked, who hated all foreigners. "It's rather bad luck on them," he went on, with bland insularity, "that the men of the European neutrals—Dutch, Danish, Norwegians or Swedes—all resemble Germans so much more than Englishmen."

The Baron turned towards Catherine and ventured upon a whispered compliment. She was wearing a wonderful pre-war dress of black velvet, close-fitting yet nowhere cramping her naturally delightful figure. A rope of pearls hung from her neck—her only ornament.

"It is permitted, Countess, to express one's appreciation of your toilette?" he ventured.

"In England it is not usual," she reminded him, with a smile, "but as you are such an old friend of the family, we will call it permissible. It is, as a matter of fact, the last gown I had from Paris. Nowadays, one thinks of other things."

"You are one of the few women," he observed, "who mix in the great affairs and yet remain intensely feminine."

"Just now," she sighed, "the great affairs do not please me."

"Yet they are interesting," he replied. "The atmosphere at the present moment is electric, charged with all manner of strange possibilities. But we talk too seriously. Will you not let me know the names of some of your guests? With General Crossley I am already acquainted."

"They really don't count for very much," she said, a little carelessly. "This is entirely aunt's Friday night gathering, and they are all her friends. That is Lady Maltenby opposite you, and her husband on the other side of my aunt."

"Maltenby," he repeated. "Ah, yes! There is one son a Brigadier, is there not? And another one sees sometimes about town—a Mr. Julian Orden."

"He is the youngest son."

"Am I exceeding the privileges of friendship, Countess," the Baron continued, "if I enquire whether there was not a rumour of an engagement between yourself and Mr. Orden, a few days ago?"

"It is in the air," she admitted, "but at present nothing is settled. Mr. Orden has peculiar habits. He disappeared from Society altogether, a few days ago, and has only just returned."

"A censor, was he not?"

"Something of the sort," Catherine assented. "He went out to France, though, and did extremely well. He lost his foot there."

"I have noticed that he uses a stick," the Baron remarked. "I always find him a young man of pleasant and distinguished appearance."

"Well," Catherine continued, "that is Mr. Braithwaiter the playwright, a little to the left—the man, with the smooth grey hair and eyeglass. Mrs. Hamilton Beardsmore you know, of course; her husband is commanding his regiment in Egypt."

"The lady on my left?"

"Lady Grayson. She comes up from the country once a month to buy food. You needn't mind her. She is stone deaf and prefers dining to talking."

"I am relieved," the Baron confessed, with a little sigh. "I addressed her as we sat down, and she made no reply. I began to wonder if I had offended."

"The man next me," she went on, "is Mr. Millson Gray. He is an American millionaire, over here to study our Y.M.C.A. methods. He can talk of nothing else in the world but Y.M.C.A. huts and American investments, and he is very hungry."

"The conditions," the Baron observed, "seem favourable for a tete-a-tete."

Catherine smiled up into his imperturbable face. The wine had brought a faint colour to her cheeks, and the young man sighed regretfully at the idea of her prospective engagement. He had always been one of Catherine's most pronounced admirers.

"But what are we to talk about?" she asked. "On the really interesting subjects your lips are always closed. You are a marvel of discretion, you know, Baron—even to me."

"That is perhaps because you hide your real personality under so many aliases."

"I must think that over," she murmured.

"You," he continued, "are an aristocrat of the aristocrats. I can quite conceive that you found your position in Russia incompatible with modern ideas. The Russian aristocracy, if you will forgive my saying so, is in for a bad time which it has done its best to thoroughly deserve. But in England your position is scarcely so comprehensible. Here you come to a sanely governed country, which is, to all effects and purposes, a country governed by the people for the people. Yet here, within two years, you have made yourself one of the champions of democracy. Why? The people are not ill-treated. On the contrary, I should call them pampered."

"You do not understand," she explained earnestly. "In Russia it was the aristocracy who oppressed the people, shamefully and malevolently. In England it is the bourgeoisie who rule the country and stand in the light of Labour. It is the middleman, the profiteer, the new capitalist here who has become an ugly and a dominant power. Labour has the means by which to assert itself and to claim its rights, but has never possessed the leaders or the training. That has been the subject of my lectures over here from the beginning. I want to teach the people how to crush the middleman. I want to show them how to discover and to utilise their strength."

"Is not that a little dangerous?" he enquired. "You might easily produce a state of chaos."

"For a time, perhaps," she admitted, "but never for long. You see, the British have one transcendental quality; they possess common sense. They are not idealists like the Russians. The men with whom I mix neither walk with their heads turned to the clouds nor do they grope about amongst the mud. They just look straight ahead of them, and they ask for what they see in the path."

"I see," he murmured. "And now, having reached just this stage in our conversation, let me ask you this. You read the newspapers?"

"Diligently," she assured him.

"Are you aware of a very curious note of unrest during the last few days—hints at a crisis in the war which nothing in the military situation seems to justify—vague but rather gloomy suggestions of an early peace?"

"Every one is talking about it," she agreed. "I think that you and I have some idea as to what it means."

"Have we?" he asked quietly.

"And somehow," she went on, dropping her voice a little, "I believe that your knowledge goes farther than mine."

He gave no sign, made no answer. Some question from across the table, with reference to the action of one of his country's Ministers, was referred to him. He replied to it and drifted quite naturally into a general conversation. Without any evident effort, he seemed to desire to bring his tete-a-tete with Catherine to a close. She showed no sign of disappointment; indeed she fell into his humour and made vigorous efforts to attack the subject of Y.M.C.A. huts with her neighbour on the right. The rest of the meal passed in this manner, and it was not until they met, an hour later, in the Princess' famous reception room, that they exchanged more than a casual word. The Princess liked to entertain her guests in a fashion of her own. The long apartment, with its many recesses and deep windows, an apartment which took up the whole of one side of the large house, had all the dignity and even splendour of a drawing-room, and yet, with its little palm court, its cosy divans, its bridge tables and roulette board, encouraged an air of freedom which made it eminently habitable.

"I wonder, Baron," she asked, "what time you are leaving, and whether I could rely upon your escort to the Lawsons' dance? Don't hesitate to say if you have an engagement, as it only means my telephoning to some friends."

"I am entirely at your service, Countess," he answered promptly. "As a matter of fact, I have already promised to appear there myself for an hour."

"You would like to play bridge now, perhaps?" she asked.

"The Princess was kind enough to invite me," he replied, "but I ventured to excuse myself. I saw that the numbers were even without me, and I hoped for a little more conversation with you."

They seated themselves in an exceedingly comfortable corner. A footman brought them coffee, and a butler offered strange liqueurs. Catherine leaned back with a little sigh of relief.

"Every one calls this room of my aunt's the hotel lounge," she remarked. "Personally, I love it."

"To me, also, it is the ideal apartment," he confessed. "Here we are alone, and I may ask you a question which was on my lips when we had tea together at the Carlton, and which, but for our environment, I should certainly have asked you at dinner time."

"You may ask me anything," she assured him, with a little smile. "I am feeling happy and loquacious. Don't tempt me to talk, or I shall give away all my life's secrets."

"I will only ask you for one just now," he promised. "Is it true that you have to-day had some disagreement with—shall I say a small congress of men who have their meetings down at Westminster, and with whom you have been in close touch for some time?"

Her start was unmistakable.

"How on earth do you know anything about that?"

He shrugged his shoulders.

"These are the days," he said, "when, if one is to succeed in my profession, one must know everything."

She did not speak for a moment. His question had been rather a shock to her. In a moment or two, however, she found herself wondering how to use it for her own advantage.

"It is true," she admitted.

He looked intently at the point of his patent shoe.

"Is this not a case, Countess," he ventured, "in which you and I might perhaps come a little closer together?"

"If you have anything to suggest, I am ready to listen," she said.

"I wonder," he went on, "if I am right in some of my ideas? I shall test them. You have taken up your abode in England. That was natural, for domestic reasons. You have shown a great interest in a certain section of the British public. It is my theory that your interest in England is for that section only; that as a country, you are no more an admirer of her characteristics than I am."

"You are perfectly right," she answered coolly.

"Your interest," he proceeded, "is in the men and women toilers of the world, the people who carry on their shoulders the whole burden of life, and whose position you are continually desiring to ameliorate. I take it that your sympathy is international?"

"It is," she assented

"People of this order in—say—Germany, excite your sympathy in the same degree?"

"Absolutely!"

"Therefore," he propounded, "you are working for the betterment of the least considered class, whether it be German, Austrian, British, or French?"

"That also is true," she agreed.

"I pursue my theory, then. The issue of this war leaves you indifferent, so long as the people come to their own?"

"My work for the last few weeks amongst those men of whom you have been speaking," she pointed out, "should prove that."

"We are through the wood and in the open, then," he declared, with a little sigh of relief. "Now I am prepared to trade secrets with you. I am not a friend of this country. Neither my Chief nor my Government have the slightest desire to see England win the war."

"That I knew," she acknowledged.

"Now I ask you for information," he continued. "Tell me this? Your pseudo-friends have presented the supposed German terms of peace to Mr. Stenson. What was the result?"

"He is taking twenty-four hours to consider them."

"And what will happen if he refuses?" the Baron asked, leaning a little towards her. "Will they use their mighty weapon? Will they really go the whole way, or will they compromise?"

"They will not compromise," she assured him. "The telegrams to the secretaries of the various Trades Unions are already written out. They will be despatched five minutes after Mr. Stenson's refusal to sue for an armistice has been announced."

"You know that?" he persisted.

"I know it beyond any shadow of doubt."

He nodded slowly.

"Your information," he admitted, "is valuable to me. Well though I am served, I cannot penetrate into the inner circles of the Council itself. Your news is good."

"And now," she said, "I expect the most amazing revelations from you."

"You shall have them, with pleasure," he replied. "Freistner has been in a German fortress for some weeks and may be shot at any moment. The supposed strength of the Socialist Party in Germany is an utter sham. The signatures attached to the document which was handed to your Council some days ago will be repudiated. The whole scheme of coming into touch with your Labour classes has been fostered and developed by the German War Cabinet. England will be placed in the most humiliating and ridiculous position. It will mean the end of the war."

"And Germany?" she gasped.

"Germany," the Baron pronounced calmly, "will have taken the first great step up the ladder in her climb towards the dominance of the world."

XIX

There were one or two amongst those present in the Council room at Westminster that evening, who noted and never forgot a certain indefinable dignity which seemed to come to Stenson's aid and enabled him to face what must have been an unwelcome and anxious ordeal without discomposure or disquiet. He entered the room accompanied by Julian and Phineas Cross, and he had very much the air of a man who has come to pay a business visit, concerning the final issue of which there could be no possible doubt. He shook hands with the Bishop gravely but courteously, nodded to the others with whom he was acquainted, asked the names of the few strangers present, and made a careful mental note of what industries and districts they represented. He then accepted a chair by the side of the Bishop, who immediately opened the proceedings.

"My friends," the latter began, "as I sent word to you a little time ago, Mr. Stenson has preferred to bring you his answer himself. Our ambassador—Mr. Julian Orden—waited upon him at Downing Street at the hour arranged upon, and, in accordance with his wish to meet you all, Mr. Stenson is paying us this visit."

The Bishop hesitated, and the Prime Minister promptly drew his chair a little farther into the circle.

"Gentlemen," he said, "the issue which you have raised is so tremendous, and its results may well be so catastrophic, that I thought it my duty to beg Mr. Orden to arrange for me to come and speak to you all, to explain to you face to face why, on behalf of His Majesty's Government, I cannot do your bidding."

"You don't want peace, then?" one of the delegates from the other side of the table asked bluntly.

"We do not," was the quiet reply. "We are not ready for it."

"The country is," Fenn declared firmly. "We are."

"So your ambassador has told me," was the calm reply. "In point of numbers you may be said, perhaps, to represent the nation. In point of intellect, of knowledge—of inner knowledge, mind—I claim that I represent it. I tell you that a peace now, even on the terms which your Socialist allies in Germany have suggested, would be for us a peace of dishonour."

"Will you tell us why?" the Bishop begged.

"Because it is not the peace we promised our dead or our living heroes," Mr. Stenson said slowly. "We set out to fight for democracy—your cause. That fight would be a failure if we allowed the proudest, the most autocratic, the most conscienceless despot who ever sat upon a throne to remain in his place."

"But that is just what we shall not do," Fenn interrupted. "Freistner has assured us of that. The peace is not the Kaiser's peace. It is the peace of the Socialist Party in Germany, and the day the terms are proclaimed, democracy there will score its first triumph."

"I find neither in the European Press nor in the reports of our secret service agents the slightest warrant for any such supposition," Mr. Stenson pronounced with emphasis.

"You have read Freistner's letter?" Fenn asked.

"Every word of it," the Prime Minister replied. "I believe that Freistner is an honest man, as honest as any of you, but I think that he is mistaken. I do not believe that the German people are with him. I am content to believe that those signatures are genuine. I will even believe that Germany would welcome those terms of peace, although she would never allow them to proceed from her own Cabinet. But I do not believe that the clash and turmoil which would follow their publication would lead to the overthrow of the German dynasty. You give me no proof of it, gentlemen. You have none yourselves. And therefore I say that you propose to work in the dark, and it seems to me that your work may lead to an evil end. I want you to listen to me for one moment," he went on, his face lighting up with a flash of terrible earnestness. "I am not going to cast about in my mind for flowery phrases or epigrams. We are plain men here together, with our country's fate in the balance. For God's sake, realise your responsibilities. I want peace. I ache for it. But there will be no peace for Europe while Germany remains an undefeated autocracy. We've promised our dead and our living to oust that corrupt monster from his throne. We've promised it to France our glorious Allies. We've shaken hands about it with America, whose ships are already crowding the seas, and whose young manhood has taken the oath which ours has taken. This isn't the time for peace. I am not speaking in the dark when I tell you that we have a great movement pending in the West which may completely alter the whole military situation. Give us a chance. If you carry out your threat, you plunge this country into revolution, you dishonour us in the face of our Allies; you will go through the rest of your lives, every one of you, with a guilt upon your souls, a stain upon your consciences, which nothing will ever obliterate. You see, I have kept my word—I haven't said much. I cannot ask for the armistice you suggest. If you take this step you threaten—I do not deny its significance you will probably stop the war. One of you will come in and take my place. There will be turmoil, confusion, very likely bloodshed. I know what the issue will be, and yet I know my duty. There is not one member of my Cabinet who is not with me. We refuse your appeal."

Every one at the table seemed to be talking at the same time to every one else. Then Cross's voice rose above the others. He rose to his feet to ensure attention.

"Bishop," he said, "there is one point in what Mr. Stenson has been saying which I think we might and ought to consider a little more fully, and that is, what guarantees have we that Freistner really has the people at the back of him, that he'll be able to cleanse that rat pit at Berlin of the Hohenzollern and his clan of junkers—the most accursed type of politician who ever breathed? We ought to be very sure about this. Fenn's our man. What about it, Fenn?"

"Freistner's letters for weeks," Fenn answered, "have spoken of the wonderful wave of socialistic feeling throughout the country. He is an honest man, and he does not exaggerate. He assures us that half the nation is pledged."

"One man," David Sands remarked thoughtfully. "If, there is a weak point about this business, which I am not prepared wholly to admit, it is that the entire job on that side seems to be run by one man. There's a score of us. I should like to hear of more on the other side."

"It is strange," Mr. Stenson pointed out, "that so little news of this gain of strength on the part of the Socialists has been allowed to escape from Germany. However rigid their censorship, copies of German newspapers reach us every day from neutral countries. I cannot believe that Socialism has made the advance Freistner claims for it, and I agree with our friends, Mr. Cross and Mr. Sands here, that you ought to be very sure that Freistner is not deceived before you take this extreme measure."

"We are content to trust to our brothers in Germany," Fenn declared.

"I am not convinced that we should be wise to do so," Julian intervened. "I am in favour of our taking a few more days to consider this matter."

"And I am against any delay," Fenn objected hotly. "I am for immediate action."

"Let me explain where I think we have been a little hasty," Julian continued earnestly. "I gather that the whole correspondence between this body and the Socialist Party in Germany has been carried on by Mr. Fenn and Freistner. There are other well-known Socialists in Germany, but from not one of these have we received any direct communication. Furthermore—and I say this without wishing to impugn in any way the care with which I am sure our secretary has transcribed these letters—at a time like this I am forced to remember that I have seen nothing but copies."

Fenn was on his feet in a moment, white with passion.

"Do you mean to insinuate that I have altered or forged the letters?" he shouted.

"I have made no insinuations," Julian replied. "At the same time, before we proceed to extremities, I propose that we spend half an hour studying the originals."

"That's common sense," Cross declared. "There's no one can object to that. I'm none so much in favour of these typewritten slips myself."

Fenn turned to whisper to Bright. Mr. Stenson rose to his feet. The glare of the unshaded lamp fell upon his strained face. He seemed to have grown older and thinner since his entrance into the room.

"I can neither better nor weaken my cause by remaining," he said. "Only let this be my parting word to you. Upon my soul as an Englishman, I believe that if you send out those telegrams to-night, if you use your hideous and deadly weapon against me and the Government, I believe that you will be guilty of this country's ruin, as you certainly will of her dishonour. You have the example of Russia before you. And I will tell you this, too, which take into your hearts. There isn't one of those men who are marching, perhaps to-night, perhaps tomorrow, to a possible death, who would thank you for trying, to save their lives or bodies at the expense of England's honour. Those about to die would be your sternest critics. I can say no more."

Julian walked with the Premier towards the door.

"Mr. Stenson," he declared, "you have said just what could be said from your point of view, and God knows, even now, who is in the right! You are looking at the future with a very full knowledge of many things of which we are all ignorant. You have, quite naturally, too, the politician's hatred of the methods these people propose. I myself am inclined to think that they are a little hasty."

"Orden," Mr. Stenson replied sternly, "I did not come to you to-night as a politician. I have spoken as a man and an Englishman, as I speak to you now. For the love of your country and her honour, use your influence with these people. Stop those telegrams. Work for delay at any cost. There's something inexplicable, sinister, about the whole business. Freistner may be an honest man, but I'll swear that he hasn't the influence or the position that these people have been led to believe. And as for Nicholas Fenn—"

The Prime Minister paused. Julian waited anxiously.

"It is my belief," the former concluded deliberately, "that thirty seconds in the courtyard of the Tower, with his back to the light, would about meet his case."

They parted at the door, and Julian returned to his seat, uneasy and perplexed. Around the Council table voices were raised in anger. Fenn, who was sitting moodily with folded arms, his chair drawn a little back from the table, scowled at him as he took his place. Furley, who had been whispering to the Bishop, turned towards Julian.

"It seems," he announced, "that the originals of most of Freistner's communications have been destroyed."

"And why not?" Fenn demanded passionately. "Why should I keep letters which would lay a rope around my neck any day they were found? You all know as well as I do that we've been expecting the police to raid the place ever since we took it."

"I am a late comer," Julian observed, "but surely some of you others have seen the original communications?"

Thomas Evans spoke up from the other end of the table,—a small, sturdily built man, a great power in South Wales.

"To be frank," he said, "I don't like these insinuations. Fenn's been our secretary from the first. He opened the negotiations, and he's carried them through. We either trust him, or we don't. I trust him."

"And I'm not saying you're not right, lad." Cross declared. "I'm for being cautious, but it's more with the idea that our German friends themselves may be a little too sanguine."

"I will pledge my word," Fenn pronounced fiercely, "to the truth of all the facts I have laid before you. Whatever my work may have been, to-day it is completed. I have brought you a people's peace from Germany. This very Council was formed for the purpose of imposing that peace upon the Government. Are you going to back out now, because a dilettante writer, an aristocrat who never did a stroke of work in his life, casts sneering doubts upon my honesty? I've done the work you gave me to do. It's up to you to finish it, I represent a million working men. So does David Sands there, Evans and Cross, and you others. What does Orden represent? Nobody and nothing! Miles Furley? A little band of Socialists who live in their gardens and keep bees! My lord Bishop? Just his congregation from week to week! Yet it's these outsiders who've come in and disturbed us. I've had enough of it and them. We've wasted the night, but I propose that the telegrams go out at eight o'clock tomorrow morning. Hands up for it!"

It was a counter-attack which swept everything before it. Every hand in the room except the Bishop's, Furley's, Cross's and Julian's was raised. Fenn led the way towards the door.

"We've our work to do, chaps," he said. "We'll leave the others to talk till daylight, if they want to."

XX

Julian and Furley left the place together. They looked for the Bishop but found that he had slipped away.

"To Downing Street, I believe," Furley remarked. "He has some vague idea of suggesting a compromise."

"Compromise!" Julian repeated a little drearily. "How can there be any such thing! There might be delay. I think we ought to have given Stenson a week—time to communicate with America and send a mission to France."

"We are like all theorists," Furley declared moodily, stopping to relight his pipe. "We create and destroy on palter with amazing facility. When it comes to practice, we are funks."

"Are you funking this?" Julian asked bluntly.

"How can any one help it? Theoretically we are right—I am sure of it. If we leave it to the politicians, this war will go dragging on for God knows how long. It's the people who are paying. It's the people who ought to make the peace. The only thing that bothers me is whether we are doing it the right way. Is Freistner honest? Could he be self-deceived? Is there any chance that he could be playing into the hands of the Pan-Germans?"

"Fenn is the man who has had most to do with him," Julian remarked. "I wouldn't trust Fenn a yard, but I believe in Freistner."

"So do I," Furley assented, "but is Fenn's report of his promises and the strength of his followers entirely honest?"

"That's the part of the whole thing I don't like," Julian acknowledged. "Fenn's practically the corner stone of this affair. It was he who met Freistner in Amsterdam and started these negotiations, and I'm damned if I like Fenn, or trust him. Did you see the way he looked at Stenson out of the corners of his eyes, like a little ferret? Stenson was at his best, too. I never admired the man more."

"He certainly kept his head," Furley agreed. "His few straight words were to the point, too."

"It wasn't the occasion for eloquence," Julian declared. "That'll come next week. I suppose he'll try and break the Trades Unions. What a chance for an Edmund Burke! It's all right, I suppose, but I wonder why I'm feeling so damned miserable."

"The fact is," Furley confided, "you and I and the Bishop and Miss Abbeway are all to a certain extent out of place on that Council.

We ought to have contented ourselves with having supplied the ideas. When it comes to the practical side, our other instincts revolt. After all, if we believed that by continuing the war we could beat Germany from a military point of view, I suppose we should forget a lot of this admirable reasoning of ours and let it go on."

"It doesn't seem a fair bargain, though," Julian sighed. "It's the lives of our men to-day for the freedom of their descendants, if that isn't frittered away by another race of politicians. It isn't good enough, Miles."

"Then let's be thankful it's going to stop," Furley declared. "We've pinned our colours to the mast, Julian. I don't like Fenn any more than you do, nor do I trust him, but I can't see, in this instance, that he has anything to gain by not running straight. Besides, he can't have faked the terms, and that's the only document that counts. And so good night and to bed," he added, pausing at the street corner, where they parted.

There was something curiously different about the demeanour of Julian's trusted servant, as he took his master's coat and hat. Even Julian, engrossed as he was in the happenings of the evening, could scarcely fail to notice it.

"You seem out of sorts to-night, Robert!" he remarked.

The latter, whose manners were usually suave and excellent, answered almost harshly.

"I have enough to make me so, sir—more than enough. I wish to give a week's notice."

"Been drinking, Robert?" his master enquired.

The man smiled mirthlessly.

"I am quite sober, sir," he answered, "but I should be glad to go at once. It would be better for both of us."

"What have you against me?" Julian asked, puzzled.

"The lives of my two boys," was the fierce reply. "Fred's gone now—died in hospital last night. It was you who talked them into soldiering."

Julian's manner changed at once, and his tone became kinder.

"You are very foolish to blame anybody, Robert. Your sons did their duty. If they hadn't joined up when they did, they would have had to join as conscripts later on."

"Their duty!" Robert repeated, with smothered scorn. "Their duty to a squirming nest of cowardly politicians—begging your pardon, sir. Why, the whole Government isn't worth the blood of one of them!"

"I am sorry about Fred," Julian said sympathetically. "All the same, Robert, you must try and pull yourself together."

The man groaned.

"Pull myself together!" he said angrily. "Mr. Orden, sir, I'm trying to keep respectful, but it's a hard thing. I've been reading the evening papers. There's an article, signed 'Paul Fiske', in the Pall Mall. They tell me that you're Paul Fiske. You're for peace, it seems—for peace with the German Emperor and his bloody crew."

"I am in favour of peace on certain terms, at the earliest possible moment," Julian admitted.

"That's where you've sold us, then—sold us all!" Robert declared fiercely. "My boys died believing they were fighting for men who would keep their word. The war was to go on till victory was won.. They died happily, believing that those who had spoken for England would keep their word. You're very soft-hearted in that article, sir, about the living. Did you think, when you sat down to write it, about the dead?—about that wilderness of white crosses out in France? You're proposing in cold blood to let those devils stay on their own dunghill."

"It is a very large question, Robert," Julian reminded him. "The war is fast reaching a period of mutual exhaustion."

The man threw all restraint to the winds.

"Claptrap!" was his angry reply. "You wealthy people want your fleshpots again. We've a few more million men, haven't we? America has a few more millions?"

"Your own loss, Robert, has made you—and quite naturally, too—very bitter," his master said gently. "You must let those who have thought this matter out come to a decision upon it. Beyond a certain point, the manhood of the world must be conserved."

"That sounds just like fine talk to me, sir, and no more; the sort of stuff that's printed in articles and that no one takes much stock of. Words were plain enough when we started out to fight this war. We were going to crush the German military spirit and not leave off fighting until we'd done it. There was nothing said then about conserving millions of men. It was to be fought out to the end, whatever it cost."

"And you were once a pacifist!"

"Pacifist!" the man repeated passionately. "Every human being with common sense was a pacifist when the war started."

"But the war was forced upon us," Julian reminded him. "You can't deny that."

"No one wishes to, sir. It was forced upon us all right, but who made it necessary? Why, our rotten government for the last twenty years! Our politicians, Mr. Julian, that are prating now of peace before their job's done! Do you think that if we'd paid our insurance like men and been prepared, this war would ever have come? Not it! We asked for trouble, and we got it in the neck. If we make peace now, we'll be a German colony in twenty years, thanks to Mr. Stenson and you and the rest of them. A man can be a pacifist all right until his head has been punched. Afterwards, there's another name for him. Is there anything more I can get you to-night before I leave, sir?"

"Nothing, thanks. I'm sorry about Fred."

Julian, conscious of an intense weariness, undressed and went to bed very soon after the man's departure. He was already in his first doze when he awoke suddenly with a start. He sat up and listened. The sound which had disturbed him was repeated,—a quiet but insistent ringing of the front-door bell. He glanced at his watch. It was barely midnight, but unusually late for a visitor. Once more the bell rang, and this time he remembered that Robert slept out, and that he was alone in the flat. He thrust his feet into slippers, wrapped his dressing gown around him, and made his way to the front door.

Julian's only idea had been that this might be some messenger from the Council. To his amazement he found himself confronted by Catherine.

"Close the door," she begged. "Come into your sitting room."

She pushed past him and he obeyed, still dumb with surprise and the shock of his sudden awakening. Catherine herself seemed unaware of his unusual costume, reckless of the hour and the strangeness of her visit. She wore a long chinchilla coat, covering her from head to foot, and a mantilla veil about her head, which partially obscured her features. As soon as she raised it, he knew that great things had happened. Her cheeks were the colour of ivory, and her eyes unnaturally distended. Her tone was steady but full of repressed passion.

"Julian," she cried, "we have been deceived—tricked! I have come to you for help. Are the telegrams sent out yet?"

"They go at eight o'clock in the morning," he replied.

"Thank God we are in time to stop them!"

Julian looked at her for a moment, utterly incredulous.

"Stop them?" he repeated. "But how can we? Stenson has declared war."

"Thank heaven for that!" she exclaimed, her voice trembling. "Julian, the whole thing is an accursed plot. The German Socialists have never increased their strength except in their own imaginations. They are absolutely powerless. This is the most cunning scheme of the whole war. Freistner has simply been the tool of the militarists. They encouraged him to put forward these proposals and to communicate with Nicholas Fenn. When the armistice has been declared and negotiations begun, the three signatures will be repudiated. The peace they mean to impose is one of their own dictation, and in the meantime we shall have created a cataclysm here. The war will never start again. All the Allies will be at a discord."

"How have you found this out?" Julian gasped.

"From one of Germany's chief friends in England. He is high up in the diplomatic service of—of a neutral country, but he has been working for Germany ever since the commencement of the war. He has been helping in this. He has seen me often with Nicholas Fenn, and he believes that I am behind the scenes, too. He believes that I know the truth, and that I am working for Germany. He is absolutely to be relied upon. Every word that I am telling you is the truth."

"What about Fenn?" Julian demanded breathlessly.

"Nicholas Fenn has had a hundred thousand pounds of German money within the last few months," she replied. "He is one of the foulest traitors who ever breathed. Freistner's first few letters were genuine enough, but for the last six weeks he has been imprisoned in a German fortress—and Fenn knows it."

"Have you any proof of all this?" Julian asked. "Remember we have the Council to face, and they are all girt for battle."

"Yes, I have proof," she answered, "indirect but damning enough. This man has sometimes forwarded and collected for me letters from connections of mine in Germany. He handed me one to-night from a distant cousin. You know him by name General Geroldberg. The first two pages are personal. Read what he says towards the end," she added, passing it on to Julian.

Julian turned up the lamp and read the few lines to which she pointed:

By the bye, dear cousin, if you should receive a shock within the next few days by hearing that our three great men have agreed to an absurd peace, do not worry. Their signatures have been obtained for some document which we do not regard seriously, and it is their intention to repudiate them as soon as a certain much-looked for event takes place. When the peace comes, believe me, it will be a glorious one for us. What we have won by the sword we shall hold, and what has been wrested from us by cunning and treachery, we shall regain.

"That man," Catherine declared, "is one of the Kaiser's intimates. He is one of the twelve iron men of Germany. Now I will tell you the name of the man with whom I, have spent the evening. It is Baron Hellman. Believe me, he knows, and he has told me the truth. He has had this letter by him for a fortnight, as he told me frankly that he thought it too compromising to hand over. To-night he changed his mind."

Julian stood speechless for a moment, his fists clenched, his eyes ablaze.

Catherine threw herself into his easy-chair and loosened her coat.

"Oh, I am tired!" she moaned. "Give me some water, please, or some wine."

He found some hock in the sideboard, and after she had drunk it they sat for some few minutes in agitated silence. The street sounds outside had died away. Julian's was the topmost flat in the block, and their isolation was complete. He suddenly realised the position.

"Perhaps," he suggested, with an almost ludicrous return to the commonplace, "the first thing to be done is for me to dress."

She looked at him as though she had noticed his dishabille for the first time. For a moment their feet seemed to be on the earth again.

"I suppose I seem to you crazy to come to you at such an hour," she said. "One doesn't think of those things, somehow."

"You are quite right," he agreed. "They are unimportant."

Then suddenly the sense of the silence, of their solitude, of their strange, uncertain relations to one another, swept in upon them both. For a moment the sense of the great burden she was carrying fell from Catherine's shoulders. She was back in a simpler world. Julian was no longer a leader of the people, the brilliant sociologist, the apostle of her creed. He was the man who during the last few weeks had monopolised her thoughts to an amazing extent, the man for whose aid and protection she had hastened, the man to whom she was perfectly content to entrust the setting right of this ghastly blunder. Watching him, she suddenly felt that she was tired of it all, that she would like to creep away from the storm and rest somewhere. The quiet and his presence seemed to soothe her. Her tense expression relaxed, her eyes became softer. She smiled at him gratefully.

"Oh, I cannot tell you," she exclaimed, "how glad I am to be with you just now! Everything in the outside world seems so terrible. Do you mind—it is so silly, but after all a woman cannot be as strong as a man, can she?—would you mind very much just holding my hand for a moment and staying here quite quietly. I have had a horrible evening, and when I came in, my head felt as though it would burst. You do not mind?"

Julian smiled as he leaned towards her. A kind of resentment of which he had been conscious, even though in some measure ashamed of it, resentment at her unswerving loyalty to the task she had set herself, melted away. He suddenly knew why he had kissed her, on that sunny morning on the marshes, an ecstatic and incomprehensible moment which had seemed sometimes, during these days of excitement, as though it had belonged to another life and another world. He took both her hands in his, and, stooping down, kissed her on the lips.

"Dear Catherine," he said, "I am so glad that you came to me. I think that during these last few days we have forgotten to be human, and it might help us—for after all, you know, we are engaged!"

"But that," she whispered, "was only for my sake."

"At first, perhaps," he admitted, "but now for mine."

Her little sigh of content, as she stole nearer to him, was purely feminine. The moments ticked on in restful and wonderful silence. Then, unwillingly, she drew away from his protecting arm.

"My dear," she said, "you look so nice as you are, and it is such happiness to be here, but there is a great task before us."

"You are right," he declared, straightening himself. "Wait for a few minutes, dear. We shall find them all at Westminster—the place will be open all night. Close your eyes and rest while I am away."

"I am rested," she answered softly, "but do not be long. The car is outside, and on the way I have more to tell you about Nicholas Fenn."

XXI

If the closely drawn blinds of the many windows of Westminster Buildings could have been raised that night and early morning, the place would have seemed a very hive of industry. Twenty men were hard at work in twenty different rooms. Some went about their labours doubtfully, some almost timorously, some with jubilation, one or two with real regret. Under their fingers grew the more amplified mandates which, following upon the bombshell of the already prepared telegrams, were within a few hours to paralyse industrial England, to keep her ships idle in the docks, her trains motionless upon the rails, her mines silent, her forges cold, her great factories empty. Even the least imaginative felt the thrill, the awe of the thing he was doing. On paper, in the brain, it seemed so wonderful, so logical, so certain of the desired result. And now there were other thoughts forcing their way to the front. How would their names live in history? How would Englishmen throughout the world regard this deed? Was it really the truth they were following, or some false and ruinous shadow? These were fugitive doubts, perhaps, but to more than one of those midnight toilers they presented themselves in the guise of a chill and drear presentiment.

They all heard a motor-car stop outside. No one, however, thought it worth while to discontinue his labours for long enough to look out and see who this nocturnal visitor might be. In a very short time, however, these labours were disturbed. From room to room, Julian, with Catherine and the Bishop, for whom they had called on the way, passed with a brief message. No one made any difficulty about coming to the Council room. The first protest was made when they paid the visit which they had purposely left until last. Nicholas Fenn had apparently finished or discontinued his efforts. He was seated in front of his desk, his chin almost resting upon his folded arms, and a cigarette between his lips. Bright was lounging in an easy-chair within a few feet of him. Their heads were close together; their conversation, whatever the subject of it may have been, was conducted in whispers. Apparently they had not heard Julian's knock, for they started apart, when the door was opened, like conspirators. There was something half-fearful, half-malicious in Fenn's face, as he stared at them.

"What are you doing here?" he demanded. "What's wrong?"

Julian closed the door.

"A great deal," he replied curtly. "We have been around to every one of the delegates and asked them to assemble in the Council room. Will you and Bright come at once?"

Fenn looked from one to the other of his visitors and remained silent for a few seconds.

"Climbing down, eh?" he asked viciously.

"We have some information to communicate," Julian announced.

Fenn moved abruptly away, out of the shadow of the electric lamp which hung over his desk. His voice was anxious, unnatural.

"We can't consider any more information," he said harshly. "Our decisions have been taken. Nothing can affect them. That's the worst of having you outsiders on the board. I was certain you wouldn't face it when the time came."

"As you yourself," Julian remarked, "are somewhat concerned in this matter, I think it would be well if you came with the others."

"I am not going to stir from this room," Fenn declared doggedly. "I have my own work to do. And as to my being concerned with what you have to say, I'll thank you to mind your own business and leave mine alone."

"Mr. Fenn," the Bishop interposed, "I beg to offer you my advice that you join us at once in the Council room."

Julian and Catherine had already left the room. Fenn leaned forward, and there was an altered note in his tone.

"What's it mean, Bishop?" he asked hoarsely. "Are they ratting, those two?"

"What we have come here to say," the Bishop rejoined, "must be said to every one."

He turned away. Fenn and Bright exchanged quick glances.

"What do you make of it?" asked Fenn.

"They've changed their minds," Bright muttered, "that's all. They're theorists. Damn all theorists! They just blow bubbles to destroy them. As for the girl, she's been at parties all the evening, as we know."

"You're right," Fenn acknowledged. "I was a fool. Come on."

Many of the delegates had the air of being glad to escape for a few minutes from their tasks. One or two of them entered the room, carrying a cup of coffee or cocoa. Most of them were smoking. Fenn and Bright made their appearance last of all. The latter made a feeble attempt at a good-humoured remark.

"Is this a pause for refreshments?" he asked. "If so, I'm on."

Julian, who had been waiting near the door, locked it. Fenn started. "What the devil's that for?" he demanded.

"Just a precaution. We don't want to be interrupted."

Julian moved towards a little vacant space at the end of the table and stood there, his hands upon the back of a chair. The Bishop remained by his side, his eyes downcast as though in prayer. Catherine had accepted the seat pushed forward by Cross. The atmosphere of the room, which at first had been only expectant, became tense.

"My friends," Julian began, "a few hours ago you came to a momentous decision. You are all at work, prepared to carry that decision into effect. I have come to see you because I am very much afraid that we have been the victims of false statements, the victims of a disgraceful plot."

"Rubbish!" Fenn scoffed. "You're ratting, that's what you are."

"You'd better thank Providence," Julian replied sternly, "that there is time for you to rat, too—that is, if you have any care for your country. Now, Mr. Fenn, I am going to ask you a question. You led us to believe, this evening, that, although all letters had been destroyed, you were in constant communication with Freistner. When did you hear from him last—personally, I mean?"

"Last week," Fenn answered boldly, "and the week before that."

"And you have destroyed those letters?"

"Of course I have! Why should I keep stuff about that would hang me?"

"You cannot produce, then, any communication from Freistner, except the proposals of peace, written within the last—say—month?"

"What the mischief are you getting at?" Fenn demanded hotly. "And what right have you to stand there and cross-question me?"

"The right of being prepared to call you to your face a liar," Julian said gravely. "We have very certain information that Freistner is now imprisoned in a German fortress and will be shot before the week is out."

There was a little murmur of consternation, even of disbelief. Fenn himself was speechless. Julian went on eagerly.

"My friends," he said, "on paper, on the facts submitted to us, we took the right decision, but we ought to have remembered this. Germany's word, Germany's signature, Germany's honour, are not worth a rap when opposed to German interests. Germany, notwithstanding all her successes, is thirsting for peace. This armistice would be her salvation. She set herself out to get it—not honestly, as we have been led to believe, but by means of a devilish plot. She professed to be overawed by the peace desires of the Reichstag. The Pan-Germans professed a desire to give in to the Socialists. All lies! They encouraged Freistner to continue his negotiations here with Fenn. Freistner was honest enough. I am not so sure about Fenn."

Fenn sprang to his feet, a blasphemous exclamation broke from his lips. Julian faced him, unmoved. The atmosphere of the room was now electric.

"I am going to finish what I have to say," he went on. "I know that every one will wish me to. We are all here to look for the truth and nothing else, and, thanks to Miss Abbeway, we have stumbled upon it. These peace proposals, which look so well on paper, are a decoy. They were made to be broken. Those signatures are affixed to be repudiated. I say that Freistner has been a prisoner for weeks, and I deny that Fenn has received a single communication from him during that time. Fenn asserts that he has, but has destroyed them. I repeat that he is a liar."

"That's plain speaking," Cross declared. "Now, then, Fenn, lad, what have you to say about it?"

Fenn leaned forward, his face distorted with something which might have been anger, but which seemed more closely to resemble fear.

"This is just part of the ratting!" he exclaimed. "I never keep a communication from Freistner. I have told you so before. The preliminary letters I had you all saw, and we deliberated upon them together. Since then, all that I have had have been friendly messages, which I have destroyed."

There was a little uncertain murmur. Julian proceeded.

"You see," he said, "Mr. Fenn is not able to clear himself from my first accusation. Now let us hear what he will do with this one. Mr. Fenn started life, I believe, as a schoolmaster at a parish school, a very laudable and excellent occupation. He subsequently became manager to a firm of timber merchants in the city and commenced to interest himself in Labour movements. He rose by industry and merit to his present position—a very excellent career, but not, I should think, a remunerative one. Shall we put his present salary down at ten pounds a week?"

"What the devil concern is this of yours?" the goaded man shouted.

"Of mine and all of us," Julian retorted, "for I come now to a certain question. Will you disclose your bank book?"

Fenn reeled for a moment in his seat. He affected not to have heard the question.

"My what?" he stammered.

"Your bank book," Julian repeated calmly. "As you only received your last instalment from Germany this week, you probably have not yet had time to purchase stocks and shares or property wherever your inclination leads you. I imagine, therefore, that there would be a balance there of something like thirty thousand pounds, the last payment made to you by a German agent now in London."

Fenn sprang to his feet. He had all the appearance of a man about to make a vigorous and exhaustive defence. And then suddenly he swayed, his face became horrible to look upon, his lips were twisted.

"Brandy!" he cried. "Some one give me brandy! I am ill!"

He collapsed in a heap. They carried him on to a seat set against the wall, and Catherine bent over him. He lay there, moaning. They loosened his collar and poured restoratives between his teeth. For a time he was silent. Then the moaning began again. Julian returned to the table.

"Believe me," he said earnestly, "this is as much a tragedy to me as to any one present. I believe that every one of you here except—" he glanced towards the sofa—"except those whom we will not name have gone into this matter honestly, as I did. We've got to chuck it. Tear up your telegrams. Let me go to see Stenson this minute. I see the truth about this thing now as I never saw it before. There is no peace for us with Germany until she is on her knees, until we have taken away all her power to do further mischief. When that time comes let us be generous. Let us remember that her working men are of the same flesh and blood as ours and need to live as you need to live. Let us see that they are left the means to live. Mercy to all of them—mercy, and all the possibilities of a free and generous life. But to Hell with every one of those who are responsible for the poison which has crept throughout all ranks in Germany, which, starting from the Kaiser and his friends, has corrupted first the proud aristocracy, then the industrious, hard-working and worthy middle classes, and has even permeated to some extent the ranks of the people themselves, destined by their infamous ruler to carry on their shoulders the burden of an unnatural, ungodly, and unholy ambition. There is much that I ought to say, but I fancy that I have said enough. Germany must be broken, and you can do it. Let the memory of those undispatched telegrams help you. Spend your time amongst the men you represent. Make them see the truth. Make them understand that every burden they lift, every time they wield the pickaxe, every blow they strike in their daily work, helps. I was going to speak about what we owe to the dead. I won't. We must beat

Germany to her knees. We can and we will. Then will come the time for generosity."

Phineas Cross struck the table with the flat of his hand.

"Boys," he said, "I feel the sweat in every pore of my body. We've nigh done a horrible thing. We are with you, Mr. Orden. But about that little skunk there? How did you find him out?"

"Through Miss Abbeway," Julian answered. "You have her to thank. I can assure you that every charge I have made can be substantiated."

There was a little murmur of confidence. Everyone seemed to find speech difficult.

"One word more," Julian went on. "Don't disband this Council. Keep it together, just as it is. Keep this building. Keep our association and sanctify it to one purpose—victory."

A loud clamour of applause answered him. Once more Cross glanced towards the prostrate form upon the sofa.

"Let no one interfere," Julian enjoined. "There is an Act which will deal with him. He will be removed from this place presently, and he will not be heard of again for a little time. We don't want a soul to know how nearly we were duped. It rests with every one of you to destroy all the traces of what might have happened. You can do this if you will. To-morrow call a meeting of the Council. Appoint a permanent chairman, a new secretary, draw out a syllabus of action for promoting increased production, for stimulating throughout every industry a passionate desire for victory. If speaking, writing, or help of mine in any way is wanted, it is yours. I will willingly be a disciple of the cause. But this morning let me be your ambassador. Let me go to the Premier with a message from you. Let me tell him what you have resolved."

"Hands up all in favour!" Cross exclaimed.

Every hand was raised. Bright came back from the couch, blinking underneath his heavy spectacles but meekly acquiescent.

"Let us remember this hour," the Bishop begged, "as something solemn in our lives. The Council of Labour shall justify itself, shall voice the will or the people, fighting for victory."

"For the Peace which comes through Victory!" Julian echoed.

XXII

The Bishop and Catherine, a few weeks later, walked side by side up the murky length of St. Pancras platform. The train which they had come to meet was a quarter of an hour late, and they had fallen into a sort of reminiscent conversation which was not without interest to both of them.

"I left Mr. Stenson only an hour ago," the Bishop observed. "He could talk about nothing but Julian Orden and his wonderful speeches. They say that at Sheffield and Newcastle the enthusiasm was tremendous, and at three shipbuilding yards on the Clyde the actual work done for the week after his visit was nearly as much again. He seems to have that extraordinary gift of talking straight to the hearts of the men. He makes them feel."

"Mr. Stenson wrote me about it," Catherine told her companion, with a little smile. "He said that no dignity that could be thought of or invented would be an adequate offering to Julian for his services to the country. For the first time since the war, Labour seems wholly and entirely, passionately almost, in earnest. Every one of those delegates went back full of enthusiasm, and with every one of them, Julian, before he has finished, is going to make a little tour in his own district."

"And after to-morrow," the Bishop remarked with a smile, "I suppose he will not be alone."

She pressed his arm.

"It is very wonderful to think about," she said quietly. "I am going to try and be Julian's secretary—whilst we are away, at any rate."

"It isn't often," the Bishop reflected, "that I have the chance of a few minutes' quiet conversation, on the day before her wedding, with the woman whom I am going to marry to the man I think most of on earth."

"Give me some good advice," she begged.

The Bishop shook his head.

"You don't need it," he said. "A wife who loves her husband needs very few words of admonition. There are marriages so often in which one can see the rocks ahead that one opens one's prayer-book, even, with a little tremor of fear. But with you and Julian it is different."

"There is nothing that a woman can do for the man whom she loves," she declared softly, "which I shall not try to do for Julian."

They paced up and down for a few moments in silence. The Bishop's step was almost buoyant. He seemed to have lost all that weary load of anxiety which had weighed him down during the last few months. Catherine, too, in her becoming grey furs, her face flushed with excitement, had the air of one who has thrown all anxiety to the winds.

"Julian's gift of speech must have surprised even himself," the Bishop remarked. "Of course, we always knew that 'Paul Fiske', when he was found, must be a brilliant person, but I don't think that even Julian himself had any suspicion of his oratorical powers."

"I don't think he had," she agreed. "In his first letter he told me that it was just like sitting down at his desk to write, except that all the dull material impedimenta of paper and ink and walls seemed rolled away, and the men to whom he wished his words to travel were there waiting. Of course, he is wonderful, but Phineas Cross, David Sands and some of the others have shown a positive genius for organisation. That Council of Socialism, Trades Unionism, and Labour generally, which was formed to bring us premature peace, seems for the first time to have brought all Labour into one party, Labour in its very broadest sense, I mean."

"The truth of the matter is," the Bishop pronounced, "that the people have accepted the dictum that whatever form of republicanism is aimed at, there must be government. A body of men who realise that, however advanced their ideas, can do but little harm. I am perfectly certain— Stenson admits it himself—that before very long we shall have a Labour Ministry. Who cares? It will probably be a good ministry—good for the country and good for the world. There has been too much juggling in international politics. This war is going to end that, once and for ever. By the bye," he went on, in an altered tone, "there is one question which I have always had in my mind to ask you. If I do so now, will you please understand that if you think it best you need not answer me?"

"Certainly," Catherine replied.

"From what source did you get your information which saved us all?"

"It came to me from a man who is dead," was the quiet answer.

The Bishop looked steadily ahead at the row of signal lights.

"There was a young foreigner, some weeks ago," he said "a Baron Hellman—quite a distinguished person, I believe—who was discovered shot in his rooms."

She acquiesced silently.

"If you were to go to the Home Office and were able to persuade them to treat you candidly, I think that you could discover some wonderful things," she confided. "I wish I could believe that the Baron was the only one who has been living in this country, unsuspected, and occupying a prominent position, who was really in the pay of Germany."

"It was a very subtle conspiracy," the Bishop remarked thoughtfully, "subtle because, in a sense, it appeared so genuine. It appealed to the very best instincts of thinking men."

"Good has come out of it, at any rate," she reminded him. "Westminster Buildings is now the centre of patriotic England. Labour was to have brought the war to an end—for Germany. It is Labour which is going to win the victory—for England."

The train rolled into the station and rapidly disgorged its crowd of passengers, amongst whom Julian was one of the first to alight. Catherine found herself trembling. The shy words of welcome which had formed themselves in her mind died away on her lips as their glances met. She lifted her face to his.

"Julian," she murmured, "I am so proud—so happy."

The Bishop left them as they stepped into their cab.

"I am going to a mission room in the neighbourhood," he explained. "We have war talks every week. I try to tell them how things are going on, and we have a short service. But before I go, Mr. Stenson has sent you a little message, Julian. If you go to your club later on to-night, you will see it in the telegrams, or you will find it in your newspapers in the morning. There has been wonderful fighting in Flanders to-day. The German line has been broken at half a dozen points. We have taken nearly twenty thousand prisoners, and Zeebrugge is threatened. Farther south, the Americans have made their start and have won a complete victory over the Crown Prince's picked troops."

The two men wrung hands.

"This," Julian declared, "is the only way to Peace."

A Note About the Author

E. Phillips Oppenheim (1866–1946) was a British writer who rose to prominence in the late nineteenth century. He was born in London to a leather merchant and began working at an early age. Oppenheim spent nearly 20 years in the family business, while juggling a freelance writing career. He composed short stories and eventually novels with more than 100 titles to his credit. His first novel, *Expiation* was published in 1886 followed by *The Mystery of Mr. Bernard Brown* (1896) and *The Long Arm of Mannister* (1910). Oppenheim is best known for his signature tales full of action and espionage.

A Note from the Publisher

Spanning many genres, from non-fiction essays to literature classics to children's books and lyric poetry, Mint Edition books showcase the master works of our time in a modern new package. The text is freshly typeset, is clean and easy to read, and features a new note about the author in each volume. Many books also include exclusive new introductory material. Every book boasts a striking new cover, which makes it as appropriate for collecting as it is for gift giving. Mint Edition books are only printed when a reader orders them, so natural resources are not wasted. We're proud that our books are never manufactured in excess and exist only in the exact quantity they need to be read and enjoyed.

bookfinity™

Discover more of your favorite classics with Bookfinity™.

- Track your reading with custom book lists.
- Get great book recommendations for your personalized Reader Type.
- Add reviews for your favorite books.
- AND MUCH MORE!

Visit **bookfinity.com** and take the fun Reader Type quiz to get started.

Enjoy our classic and modern companion pairings!

Printed in the USA
CPSIA information can be obtained
at www.ICGtesting.com
JSHW082339140824
68134JS00020B/1767

9 781513 281247